DAWN RYDER
Improper

ELLORA'S CAVE
ROMANTICA PUBLISHING

An Ellora's Cave Romantica Publication

www.ellorascave.com

Improper

ISBN 9781419955631
ALL RIGHTS RESERVED.
Improper Pursuits Copyright © 2005 Dawn Ryder
Improper Lessons Copyright © 2005 Dawn Ryder
Edited by Sue-Ellen Gower
Cover art by Syneca

Trade paperback Publication April 2007

Excerpt from *Improper Longings* Copyright © Dawn Ryder, 2006

Content Advisory:

S – ENSUOUS
E – ROTIC
X – TREME

Ellora's Cave Publishing offers three levels of Romantica™ reading entertainment: S (S-ensuous), E (E-rotic), and X (X-treme).

The following material contains graphic sexual content meant for mature readers. This story has been rated E-rotic.

S-*ensuous* love scenes are explicit and leave nothing to the imagination.

E-*rotic* love scenes are explicit, leave nothing to the imagination, and are high in volume per the overall word count. E-rated titles might contain material that some readers find objectionable — in other words, almost anything goes, sexually. E-rated titles are the most graphic titles we carry in terms of both sexual language and descriptiveness in these works of literature.

X-*treme* titles differ from E-rated titles only in plot premise and storyline execution. Stories designated with the letter X tend to contain difficult or controversial subject matter not for the faint of heart.

Also by Dawn Ryder

ဆာ

Talon's Trophy
Tempting A Lady
Hawk's Prey
Reaching Back
Improper Longings

About the Author

ဆာ

Dawn welcomes comments from readers. You can find her website and email address on her author bio page at www.ellorascave.com.

CONTENTS

ഏ

Improper Pursuits

~9~

Improper Lessons

~107~

IMPROPER PURSUITS

ဿ

Chapter One

ஒ

The pursuit of perfection could fill a lifetime. It was simply too bad that the endless hours of preparation, training and practice failed to deliver any true reward of happiness.

The mirror was polished to a gleaming perfection and the image reflected was so very correct. Lynette sent her riding crop snapping into her skirt as her lips turned into a most improper pout. She turned away from the reflection of ladylike perfection as she forced her lips to smooth into a calm expression.

Her two maids bobbed quick curtsies as she passed. Lady Lynette Edwardmoore was everything her parents had ever wanted her to be. Poised and polished and married to a man of standing in the Boston society of 1885.

Widowed, she corrected herself. Still, she had managed to fulfill her mother's wishes along with her father's expectations in her first season. It was rather unfortunate that her late husband had such an addiction to fast horses, but then men often met their end during foolish displays of courage.

Lynette sighed under her breath as she carefully descended the stairs to the bottom floor of the house. Her riding habit was far easier to manage than an evening dress but it did require some attention. Not even the hint of an ankle was proper to show and the skirts were hemmed to just a bare inch above her toes. But there was no bustle attached to her bottom, only a small quilted horsehair pad, making walking far simpler than the rest of the day's wardrobe would demand. A lady simply didn't appear in public with a natural bottom.

Lynette felt her heart begin to accelerate as she neared the bottom of the stairs. Riding was her only escape from the constrictions of ladyship. At least when she was mounted on a steed, there wasn't the ever-present need to think about her expression. Even a lady didn't need to be mild while she rode!

Stepping out of the back door, she lifted her nose. The morning was fresh, filling her lungs with the sweet smell of life. The stables were a short walk from the main house. Housed inside the large out-building were the two mares that her departed husband had gifted her with. Paul had loved to breed horses, it had been his passion. It was the one thing Lynette truly enjoyed about him. In fact, it was the only topic they'd ever held a conversation about.

Walking towards the building, Lynette entered through the side door. Instead of the hush that normally filled the stalls, this morning there were two voices echoing through the straw and dust.

"Sanders! You're a wicked pepper, to be certain!"

"Aye, and you keep coming back for a nip from the hottest pepper you've ever tasted!"

There was a sharp gasp and a giggle. Lynette stood in the aisleway as she considered what she heard. The oddest sounds drifted from the back room. She shouldn't pry, but with no one about to critique her behavior, the temptation to indulge her curiosity was too much.

Casting a quick look about, Lynette grabbed her skirt and pulled it a foot off the ground as she followed the sounds. Creeping along the stalls, she peeked around the corner into the stable master's workroom.

Her jaw and her skirt both dropped as she took in the stable master. The man was at his workbench, however his labor was not what she would have expected to discover him doing. His breath was hard as he labored between the spread thighs of one of Lynette's maids.

She should be horrified. Her mother would be. Instead, her heart beat with a frantic pace as Lynette stared in fascination at the display. There was the slap of flesh as

Sanders rammed his body forward. Soft wet sounds came when he pulled out of the maid's spread body. His hands gripped her hips and raised them for his actions.

It was wicked and horrible, but her eyes were glued to the bounce of Sanders' bannocks as he drove his rigid erection back and forth between his consort's legs. A tingle of pleasure shot right down into Lynette's belly as she watched the swollen penis leave the maid's body and be pushed back into it.

"Aye, Heather, take my old boy. He'll make you spend again."

Heather simply gasped and wiggled as she pushed her bottom up for that engorged penis. Her head was thrown back as she gasped and moaned. Lynette bit into her gloved hand as she watched the pure enjoyment cross the woman's face.

"Harder! Harder!"

Sanders rammed his body forward in response. His face was washed with enjoyment as he watched his partner. Heather suddenly froze and jerked as Sanders shoved his penis deeply into her body. A deep moan rose from her body as she appeared to shudder. Her legs twisted around the stable master as she used them to hold him in place. It appeared almost like she enjoyed him penetrating her body.

Confusion swept through Lynette as she watched. That moan wasn't one born from pain. Instead, it sounded like a sigh of deep pleasure. While Paul had certainly done his duty by her in the marriage bed, there had never been any such activity between her own thighs. It had all been done so very gently.

"Well now! I've got to get back to work." Heather pushed Sanders away from her body. Lynette stared in fascination at the spread female flesh exposed now that the stable master wasn't between Heather's legs. She had never even dared to touch her genitals and now she could see what had always been instilled in her as a forbidden place.

Sanders stood there with his penis stiffly swollen as Heather sighed before forcing herself to slip down from the workbench. She fumbled with the buttons on her top as she aimed a smile at Sanders. She sighed before reaching forward to curl her hand around Sanders' swollen sex. She gripped the rod and moved her hand down the length of it.

"You've got the hardest cock I ever did touch. Does it ever slack?"

Sanders laughed deeply before he delivered a kiss to the maid's lips. "Not often. Are you sure you have to go? I could fuck that sweet pussy for another hour."

A smile appeared on Heather's face before she stretched up on her toes to plant a kiss on Sanders' mouth. Her fingers were still stroking up and down the length of the man's penis as she pressed her mouth to his. He appeared to suck on her mouth as his hand cradled the back of her head in place.

"Well, I'll be back for that fucking when dinner's been cleared, for certain. But I can't have the mistress noticing I'm missing. Lose my posting, I would. She's a cold fish to be sure."

She scurried away as Lynette felt disappointment hit her. Her body was alive with a pulse of sensation. Excitement surged through her, making her hot. There was the oddest throb in her passage.

Sanders suddenly froze. His face turned hard as his eyes cut straight through the dim light. He didn't frantically strive to cover his body. Instead, he inclined his head as his eyes locked with hers.

"Morning, my lady."

Lynette straightened up but didn't turn her eyes away from him. She might be many things, but she wasn't a coward. A single corner of Sanders' mouth twitched up as she returned his gaze.

"Aren't ladies expected to blush or some nonsense thing like that?"

A naughty smile lifted her lips as Lynette let her eyes wander over his penis again. She had never really looked at a man's weapon before. Strange thing that. Her husband had pushed his unseen into her tender flesh. It seemed rather natural to know what one looked like.

Sanders laughed. His chest shook as he tossed his head back. He lifted the pole of his sex with a large hand and stroked it.

"Go on and look your fill. I never did understand why the upper crust finds such things so disturbing. It's just a cock."

Indeed it was. Lynette watched the way the skin moved as his fingers stroked it. His grip was firm, just like Heather's had been. The head of the thing was ruby red and had a small slit at its top. A drop of fluid appeared as his hands moved from the base to the tip and back. Two sacs hung below the rod. The skin there was loose and red.

"Heather said your husband fucked you with all his clothes on. I see she's not a liar."

"You just fornicated with Heather with your shirt on as well."

Lynette slapped a hand over her mouth. She was mad! She should have fainted, or run, or screamed, not stood there watching them mate! There had to be something wrong with her because she simply returned her eyes to his cock and the second drop of fluid that appeared on its head.

"She was hot and didn't have the time to be waiting for me to take her back to my bed."

"Oh." It was such a simple sound. Lynette lifted her eyes to Sanders' face. He was plainly speaking to her of frank matters. Such a strange thing. It had taken her mother great effort to explain the marriage bed to her. Yet here she stood with a man who didn't find the topic uncomfortable. Nor was the man concerned about displaying his bare...cock.

"What do you mean, hot?" She shouldn't have asked the question, but frankly, Lynette didn't care. She was so listless, life was so boring. Watching Heather take that huge cock into her body had been exciting. At that very moment, she wanted to find the courage to touch that hard penis herself and discover what the thing felt like clasped in her own bare fingers.

Sanders grunted in response. He reached for the trousers that were pooled around his ankles and pulled them into place. Lynette felt her face fall into a frown as his weapon disappeared from her sight. The rush the forbidden view had given her made her tingle. It was like a secret that everyone she'd ever known had kept from her. She was eager to keep the excitement flowing through her veins.

"I don't understand you gentlefolks." Sanders began stuffing his shirt into the newly fastened trousers. "Don't see why a lady should be expected to act like she's not a woman. You've got all the same parts, blue blood, money or not."

Lynette bit her lip but still hesitated instead of leaving. Everyone whispered about the "base" needs of a man. Did that mean women had such urges? Sanders seemed to think that Heather did.

Curiosity refused to release her as Sanders rubbed a large hand over his jaw and considered her. His eyes were rather sharp as they ran down her entire body. It was a blatant look that her governess had warned her men employed when they were being base. But Lynette found she really didn't mind the look. The tingle returned to her belly as Sanders looked back at her face.

"Well, my lady, you must be the boldest gentlewoman I ever have met. Don't be dismissing little Heather. She's not immoral."

"I didn't think she was." But she should have. Servants were dismissed for far less. Her mother had dismissed footmen for simply looking at her dressing maids.

"You didn't? Well now, maybe you might just have a bit of courage. Most ladies of your breeding don't have a scrap of it. I hear your mother is afraid of her own body."

"What do you mean?"

Sanders propped a hand on the workbench and gave her a hard look. He was torn.

The line between servant and lady was a very thick one but Lynette felt perched on the edge of discovery. She seemed to yearn for the knowledge that had somehow never been taught to her. Truly she understood that the man was being harsh in an effort to get her to leave. He intended to shock her, yet Lynette felt excitement rising instead of distaste.

Sanders grunted again before he smiled at her. "Master's wife bathes in a dress and faints if she sees her own tits. That doctor comes up to the house once a week to treat her for her maladies. Do you know what that means?"

She did. Lynette felt her eyes grow wide because she'd never thought there was a sane woman on the face of the earth who would allow that to happen to her. Science called it treatment, but Lynette wasn't certain it was natural to need something like that.

"Aye. That so-called doctor brings his tools up and futters her with them until she spends. All she needs is a good fucking from her husband. Ain't nothing about that that needs a doctor."

"I hear there are ladies that find it most comforting."

Lynette knew there were many ladies who had such visits. Indeed, they looked forward to them. She didn't. She just didn't see why they might enjoy having their bodies penetrated more often than their husbands might demand. Hearing that her own mother paid for like treatments was shocking but not in a horrible manner. Lynette found it highly interesting.

But Heather seemed to enjoy it also. Lynette considered the pulse and throb inside her belly. The truth was it was in her passage, not her belly. A very odd thing to notice. It was a part of her body that she'd been taught to ignore.

"You should be on your way, lady."

"Yes, I will."

"You don't sound too happy." Sander's eyes wandered over the swell of her breasts as a corner of his mouth lifted.

"I enjoyed the conversation."

A full smile appeared on Sanders' face before he lifted an eyebrow. "Well, I'd invite you back, but I don't think you'd take me up on the invitation."

She would! In a heartbeat! Excitement filled the workroom as well as something that made her very skin feel alive. Lynette couldn't wait for a reason to return to the stables. Tomorrow morning's daily ride seemed an eternity away.

"I'd be delighted to return."

"Don't be." Sanders stuck a single finger out at her. "I'm not one of your whey-faced gentlemen callers. I want to do a whole lot more than talk to you. So just keep your white-gloved hands away from my workroom. I prefer women visitors. Ladies don't have no place here."

Lynette lifted her hand to stare at her glove. It was marred with a dark stain from her own lips. She felt so empty as she turned to leave. In front of her stretched out the endless hours of emptiness that made up her day. Oh, indeed there were tasks aplenty to do but nothing that would make her very blood surge and her heart pound.

She looked back at the stable master. He was a large man, his shoulders coated with thick muscle from his labor. But all she could think about was the huge weapon that was covered by his trousers. An insane urge to stroke it entered her head and her passage immediately pulsed with the idea. Lynette wanted to handle that penis exactly like Heather had done. Maybe then she would understand what made the other girl moan with such rapture.

Temptation mocked her with the knowledge that she was free to indulge her curiosity. She was a widow and one who had completed her mourning time. Right then her mother was once again plotting another season to end in a second marriage. However, in the meantime, she answered to no one, save God.

"Tell me what you would do with me other than talk."

Sanders shook his head. He was hearing things. But she was standing in the doorway, her eyes alight with passion. He was insane to even suggest such a thing but she just looked so hungry.

She was a pretty little thing with golden hair and blue eyes. She was strapped into a tiny corset that pushed her bosom up. He couldn't see an inch of her legs but he bet they were plump and delightful. She should be crumpled on the ground in horror. Instead, she was asking what he might like to do. Still, there was one sure way to discover if she truly had a backbone or not.

"I'd like to lay you out on my table and bare your legs for me."

"You want to see my legs?"

It was the damnedest thing he'd ever seen. She didn't blink, but considered his question instead. She raised her blue eyes to look into his face. "Why?"

"Because a woman's legs are amazing. I love to touch them."

"My husband never touched my legs."

"Not even as he rode you?"

Lynette considered that question. What Sanders wanted to do seemed vastly different from the rather sterile actions of her husband in their bed. Her husband had referred to her as quite pleasant.

"Not with his hands."

"More the fool him."

Sanders' hand absently rubbed the bulge of his cock as his eyes moved over her body again. He liked what he saw and it wasn't the pleasant way that gentlemen had always looked at her. This was…base.

"Why do you say that? He performed his duties."

Sanders laughed again. This time he seemed unable to control the waves of amusement. They shook his body and he bent over to brace his hands onto his thighs as he continued to laugh. Tears sparkled in his eyes when he finally recovered himself.

"There are a lot of things in life that are demands, but being duty-bound to ride between your sweet legs certainly isn't one of them."

Her skin suddenly caught fire. Lynette almost moaned as she felt the surge of feeling race towards her deepest center. An image of her body lying on the workbench sent her lungs into a frantic need to fill. Sanders became quiet as he watched her face.

"Aye, I'd enjoy riding you, no doubt. I bet you're wet after watching me give Heather a good pounding."

"Wet?" Lynette began to feel quite foolish for not understanding his terms. Although, as she felt the heat radiate from her own skin, she certainly understood "hot" now.

"Aye, 'wet'. Is your pussy wet now that you're as hot as Heather was?" Sanders offered a sarcastic grin as he patted the workbench. "If you've got the courage, I'd be happy to show you what a base man does with his woman."

He was testing her. Lynette knew it. The stable master expected her to flee in the face of his crudity. Yet…was it all so very crude? Her heart was racing and her blood almost boiling as she dropped her eyes to the bulge in the front of his trousers.

Behaving correctly certainly hadn't filled her with the happiness everyone declared life should be. Indeed, Heather's moan was echoing inside her head as she bit her lip and longed for a taste of whatever had made the maid so blissful. To be completely correct, she did not belong to any man right then. Her mourning was just barely complete and she would not receive callers until she appeared at the first social event of the season.

"All right." Lynette yanked her skirt away from her feet and stepped forward. Sanders fell back from her but quickly caught himself. A smile lifted his lips before he stepped up to take her challenge. His fingers threaded through her hair to grip her head. Warm breath hit her lips as his eyes seemed to trace their outline.

"Do you know what you're doing?"

"No. I believe we have established the fact that I am ignorant."

A kiss couldn't hurt. Sanders lowered his mouth and took the tempting innocence offered to him. She was sweet and soft. The scent of her hair made him itch with need. Her lips parted under the insistence of his tongue and he thrust forward to taste her.

The earth fell out from beneath her feet. Lynette thrust her arms forward and clung to Sanders as he stroked her tongue with his. Delicious sensation exploded inside her as she rose on her tiptoes to get closer to him. Such a torment of pleasure flowed from their joined lips. It was exciting, yet it left her yearning for something much deeper.

His hands curled around her hips and lifted her. The workbench was hard beneath her bottom, and cool air suddenly rushed across her legs as her skirt was swept aside. A bolt of pleasure shot into her belly as she opened her eyes to see Sanders looking at her legs. His face was harsh yet cut with appreciation. He reached for her thigh and smoothed a firm hand up its length.

Lynette fell back upon her elbows as he stroked along her leg and then up the inside of it. The fabric of her drawers suddenly felt harsh, like it was riddled with burrs.

"Take them off."

A dark eyebrow lifted. "Aye, lady, that I will."

A sharp tug and he stripped the garment away. It wasn't exposing. Instead, Lynette stared at the expression on Sanders' face. His eyes were glued to her body. His fingers stretched towards her bare skin and she moaned as he stroked her like the finest of china silk.

His hand suddenly came back to her knees and pulled them apart. It was another test of her will. Lynette looked into his face as he raised his eyebrow in question. Both his hands gently parted her thighs and spread them widely. It was faintly overwhelming but exciting too. He couldn't seem to keep his eyes on her face. He looked at the flesh he'd bared and grunted.

"Aye, you are wet. Tempting beyond compare with your little bottom just peeking out at me."

"Make me moan like Heather did." She wanted it terribly in that moment. Her passage was shouting with need. Letting her thighs fall even farther apart, she waited for him to free his weapon for her.

"Well, there's more than one way to do that. Maybe we'll start with a taste."

"Taste?"

"You're a curious one, aren't you?"

Lynette nodded as he stroked her thighs again. There was so much she wanted to know. So much she needed to feel. Right then her body was more alive than she could ever remember and she embraced the waves of sensation with open arms. It was a stolen moment and rich with excitement. Here was a chance to feel something buried deep inside her own body. She might not know what it was but she craved a taste of that forbidden treat before society imprisoned her behind its proper rules and dictates.

Before she bowed to her parents' will and married again.

"Well now. This is wet." A single fingertip touched her sex. Fire flared from the point as her hips jerked. Sanders smiled as he applied the same finger to her body and slipped it into her passage.

"Very wet." The finger left as Lynette pushed her body back towards it. Her passage wanted to clench around it. Needing the hard presence inside her. Instead, he ran the finger along the folds of her sex, bringing a new rush of fluid from her body. Her head fell back as sensation became searing. Everything seemed to center under that single thick finger. She wanted and twisted as her body demanded.

He thrust the finger completely within her and she groaned. Her body pulsed as the passage clenched around him. It felt so good there inside her, as if she'd been empty

"That husband of yours was an idiot. To have a hot pussy at his command and never do anything with it."

"He did his duty."

The finger left, making her whimper. She wanted more. Lynette lifted her eyes and raised her head. She wanted that huge penis inside her. Her body demanded it and she didn't care about anything else.

"Nay, lady, he serviced you like a cow. This wet pussy was made for hours of fucking. The kind of fucking that drains the body and leaves you panting." Sanders leaned forward until she felt the brush of his breath across her spread sex. Lynette watched with amazement as he sent his tongue out to lap up the very center of her body. Her hips bucked and he tightened his grip. A low laugh rumbled out of his chest before he licked her again and settled his mouth over her sex. The tip of his tongue flicked over her, making her squirm before he sucked on her. There was a tiny nub hidden in her folds that he centered the attention on. Every nerve in her body drew into a single knot as he sucked harder and harder on the little nub.

She moaned exactly as Heather had done.

The sound rose out of her body without her help. The pleasure was almost painful with its intensity. Her lungs burned for air as she struggled to lift her chest. Every muscle was heavy as her heart pounded in her ears. The soft lap of his tongue wrung a final few waves of pleasure from her before he lifted his head to grin at her. It was a smug expression.

"That's tasting, darling." He pressed her legs together and sent her rolling from the workbench. A sharp slap landed on her bare bottom, making her complete the journey to her feet.

"Now, go away before I open my drawers and give you the fucking your sweet little pussy needs."

Chapter Two

❧

They had guests tonight. Lynette frowned as she watched her maids begin laying out her evening dress. She didn't want to be laced and buttoned into fashion's latest creations. Her body wanted to be free to indulge itself.

She sighed as the chair in front of her dressing table was pulled out for her. There were appearances to keep up. Considering her face, she felt a smile melt her frown. Her cheeks were alight with color and her eyes sparkled. Guilt should have shown up with shame in tow, yet all she felt was the steady surge of discovery.

Who would have known that her body held places that could yield such delight? Would she ever have believed that her body could erupt with sensation other than pain during sex? It was a topic worth considering. No one had ever breathed a single word that might have hinted that marriage duty could be pleasurable.

"You're lovely tonight, my lady."

"Thank you, Janet."

There were tiny gasps that were smothered behind quickly raised hands as she used the maid's first name so freely. Lynette smiled brightly. She was dreadfully tired of the staunch need to observe her position above everyone in the house. What did it matter here in her private dressing room?

She was lovely in lavender brocade that draped perfectly over her bustle. The things were back in style with a vengeance a bare year after the "natural form" had banished all manner of shaped undergarments. Turning to look at her back, Lynette admired the slim line her corset helped to make. She did like her corset. It shaped her waist so nicely.

And she did so enjoy being out of black! Two years of mourning were expected, but she detested them. Why was she expected to weep for a man she barely knew? Paul had been more her father's friend than hers.

Janet pulled the last button through its hole on her glove and stepped away from her mistress. Lynette smiled at the girl and turned towards the door. Suddenly the night felt promising. There would be music and her feet itched to dance. Her mother expected the season to end in another marriage and maybe it would. Lynette didn't much care beyond the fact that she could join the dancing once again.

Widowhood restrictions had bored her nearly to death! No dancing, no jewelry, no callers, and black and purple to wear day in and out. Sitting at home while the carriages passed beneath her window on their way to gala events where all her friends were and she was forbidden to attend for a full year. The following year, only sedate events had been allowed such as christenings and afternoon bridal showers.

Well, that was over at last!

The ballroom was full. Lynette scanned the faces of upper society and bit her lip to keep her amusement hidden. She hadn't noticed how truly boring most of them were. Mothers sat on vigilant guard as their daughters were allowed only the briefest of greetings from gentlemen.

Lynette felt her lips twitch. Laced and buttoned as they all were, exactly what did those mothers think could happen?

"Lynette, my dear. Would you care to join me tonight?"

Lynette turned with wide eyes. Lady Celeste Blackstone stood in perfect position as she waited for a reply. Lynette dropped the quickest of curtsies and Celeste smiled at her.

Lady Celeste had always been so vastly removed from Lynette's world. She seemed to radiate grace. Yet it was so much more than that. Men adored Lady Celeste. They clamored for her attention, and no one knew just why.

Lynette had spent hours at dances watching the way the lady used her eyes to entice her companions. Everyone whispered about her, yet there was still nothing improper about her actions. It was simply the allure that lightened her eyes, it made her so very seductive.

Gentlemen's eyes clung to their steps as Celeste began a slow promenade of the room. It was a moment that showed her off to perfection. Lynette smiled as she let her body fall into the flow of motion. Her blood began to speed along as she enjoyed the stares. Somehow, being content with herself made the heart lift.

"I'm rather pleasantly surprised to see marriage suiting you so well, Lynette."

It was a bare whisper. Celeste kept her eyes on the room as she spoke out of the corner of her mouth. She moved her eyes and let them move over Lynette's face. There was a depth of knowledge inside those eyes. Lynette suddenly understood why Celeste commanded so much attention. This lady was no fool.

"Oh my." Celeste lifted Lynette's chin with her gloved hand and stared into her eyes. "I see. You really must miss your husband."

Lynette struggled to keep her face calm because Celeste was watching her with sharp eyes. A tiny fear collided with her newfound excitement. If anyone found out about that morning, she'd be ruined forever. Society was one hundred percent unforgiving. Her parents could dump her in the street in her shift and no one would interfere. With no child born from their union, she had been left with only widow's thirds and that was controlled by her father.

That was no great amount of money. Without a child to inherit, the next blood relative had. By law, she only got a third of one half of the estate income. The house she had been mistress of now belonged to a younger brother as did the stables and horse stock. Her sister-in-law was mistress of the estate now. So Lynette had been packed off to return to her father's home like unwanted baggage.

Celeste snapped her fan open and fluttered it in front of her face. She leaned behind the cream-colored paper and glared sharply at Lynette. "Don't be a ninny. If you want to live your life in fear, go join the other ladies in their endless prattle over hair ornaments."

"I much prefer your company, Celeste."

The fan snapped shut. "Let's take a turn in the garden. I adore the smell of jasmine."

Celeste sent a sharp look about as they made the last aisle in the garden. She turned her sharp eyes around and dropped the sweetly smiling face that she always presented to society. Instead, she looked at Lynette with a face that was alight with excitement.

"So if your husband was an idiot hiding behind the title of gentleman, then who found the courage to teach you about life?"

It was a very dangerous question to answer, even to ask. Lynette considered Celeste as she realized why the woman radiated such passion. This lady had also explored the joys of being a woman.

"I believe my studies in this matter have been somewhat limited." Lynette considered her desire to handle Sanders' cock. Just seeing the ruby-headed weapon wasn't enough.

"Did your husband actually make you spend?"

Lynette laughed. Paul hadn't even made her hot! "I caught one of the maids in the stable and…"

Celeste snapped her fan against her skirt and took another sharp look about. "Don't tell me you just watched. That has its own rewards, but I see it in your eyes. Did you join them?"

Celeste wasn't shocked. Instead, she appeared to enjoy waiting for the story. Her eyes sparkled as she gave Lynnette her complete attention. Lynette felt her blood heat as she recalled the morning. Finding a kindred soul made it so much better.

Celeste hummed under her breath as she listened. "Do yourself a favor, Lynette. Remember how that felt and don't let your mother marry you off to some cold fish. It feels ten times better when a cock makes you spend."

"Really? Can a husband truly do that, I mean a gentleman husband?"

"Mine does." Celeste began a slow pace that would take them back to the drawing room. "Lynette dear. You can be one of two things in this life. One of those discarded wives in there, or you can twist your husband around your little finger. Men are firmly attached to their genitals. They want a lady on their arm but a pair of lips wrapped around their cocks after the bed curtains are pulled. Take my advice and be both the wife and the mistress."

Lady Celeste's husband parted from the crowd the second his wife appeared in the doorway. Celeste aimed a lowered look at Lynette that was full of heat. "I am having a summer party and you must come. You'll be delighted by some of my guests."

Celeste held her arm out to her husband. "George dear, I'm suddenly very fatigued."

Lynette watched the flutter of Celeste's eyelashes and the thin tide of red that appeared on her husband's neck above his collar. She pushed her lips into a tiny pout that made him shift before firmly laying her arm onto his. Celeste shot Lynette a wicked smile from beneath her lowered head before her husband made a round of hasty farewells.

The rest of the gentlemen were oblivious to Lynette herself. It would surprise Lynette to discover if any of her mother's guests had noticed her exit from the room at all. With brandy in hand, they stood with their friends as they shut out the endless chatter of the wives and ladies in the room, while Celeste's husband hung upon her each and every word.

Determination fired her blood as she watched Celeste depart. Without a doubt, the other lady would be moaning with delight tonight and Lynette wanted her share of life's bliss. Society didn't need to know. Wicked temptation called to her as she decided to accept Celeste's invitation. Her mother wouldn't disapprove and the look the lady had given her promised…oh…she didn't know but she was practically desperate to discover what felt better than having Sanders taste her.

And she would not be joining the hair ornament discussions!

* * * * *

"You are toying with me, darling." George pulled the tips of his gloves free before tossing one of his white hand coverings onto the seat next to him. Inside their carriage, he let his eyes roam over his wife's breasts freely.

"I am not." Celeste smiled coyly at her husband before she pulled the hem of her skirt up to her knees. George's eyes dropped instantly to the black stockings covering her legs. He licked his lower lip, making her breath lodge in her throat as she thought about what he might do with that tongue.

"I invited her to share our anniversary celebration." George's eyes shot back to her face as a frown marred his face. "I am not wrong, dear little Lynette is quite our type of company. We really must help her find a proper husband. Admit you want a taste of her."

George flushed before he left the carriage seat and knelt before her. His large hands pushed her skirts up her thighs before he spread them wide. "What I want is a taste of you." He pressed her thighs open as he pulled her bottom to the very edge of the seat. Celeste flung her hand back to hold onto the back of the seat as her husband licked her open slit. A sigh of pleasure filled the carriage as he reached the top of her clit and sucked her little bud into his mouth. The tip of his tongue flickered over the button like lightning that shot up into her womb. The sound of the horses covered her moans as her husband sucked and then licked down her folds to her opening.

"That is what I crave, wife, your cries as I teach you who your master is." Celeste hissed at her husband as the carriage bounced beneath her bottom. George trailed a single finger through the folds of her sex before looking at her face again. "It's a rather long trip home, my dear, are you sure you want to question my will?" Little wet sounds hit her ears as he thrust that finger into her pussy. Pleasure and need twisted in her as she lifted her hips towards deeper penetration.

"I will always meet you on the field, George. Admit you enjoy the battle as much as I do and fuck me."

Her husband chuckled and pulled his finger out of her body. A few rustles of fabric told her he was freeing his cock and a second later he pulled her onto the opposite seat with him. His hands lifted her bottom and the head of his cock pressed against the opening to her pussy. Celeste cried with pleasure as she settled her thighs on either side of George's hips and lowered her body onto his cock.

"I enjoy long rides."

Her husband groaned as she matched the bounce of the carriage. Up and down, she rode his cock, making sure not to ride him too fast. She always got delightfully wet when George sucked her pussy and now she wanted to savor the thrust of his hard cock inside her. The idea that she might have discovered a new friend fired her passion even more.

Moving faster, Celeste listened to her husband's moans and moved her bottom faster. Pleasure threatened to take her with its grip but she resisted as she worked her hips faster. George grunted as his fingers dug into her hips and he groaned as his cock pumped hot seed up into her womb.

Celeste cried out as she ground her pussy down onto his cock. Pleasure jerked her in its claws as she cried out. George caught her body and stroked his hands over her back as she enjoyed the afterglow of their intimacy. His cock was still hard inside her, promising her a long night.

Celeste lifted her head from her husband's shoulder and smiled. "You did say Nigel would be coming?"

George lifted an eyebrow and his cock twitched inside her. "Hungry, darling? You don't need to make excuses to get Nigel to join us."

Celeste watched the flare of heat cross her husband's eyes. His hands lifted her hips and let her slip back down his cock. Society would never forgive her if they discovered how very much she loved her husband. That was so exceedingly unfashionable. Discovering that little flaw had been the beginning of her downfall, now she craved the dark pleasures moments like this offered her.

The hard thrust of his cock stretching her pussy. The taste of his seed when she sucked his cock. There were a hundred wicked secrets that she had shared with him and she hungered for even more.

Limits were for the outside world and its strict codes of morality. Love granted her a haven of freedom where she might enjoy the body her soul was attached to. "I miss Nigel."

George chuckled before lifting up from his seat and dropping her bottom onto her abandoned seat. Her thighs were spread wide by his hips as he began fucking her with hard thrusts. No jealousy crossed his face as his cock thrust deeply into her. Her husband watched her with hard eyes as he held her hips in place for his fucking. "I'm delighted to hear that, Celeste."

* * * * *

Morning didn't come soon enough. Lynette looked at the bellpull next to her bed and sighed. It wasn't even dawn yet. But she couldn't sleep. Her body seemed to be slowly burning. The difference today was she now knew what she craved.

She could feel the smooth slide of fluid between her legs. The sun crept across the horizon slowly as she wandered the length of her room. Her night dress frustrated her with its high collar and endless fabric. The dawn air brushed her cheeks, tempting her with its chill.

How much more intense it must feel to have the body uncovered. Casting a look about, Lynette worried her lower lip as she walked towards the door and gave the bolt a push. She turned to stare at the bed she had used as a virgin and now once again slept in. Was she changed due to Paul's visits to her bed? His attendance in the bed chamber had been staunch and proper and she had been his obedient little child bride.

A naughty smile lifted her lips as her fingers found the buttons on her nightdress. Lynette opened the yoke of the garment before her fingers grasped the billowing skirt and pulled the hateful thing over her head. She grasped her drawers and pulled them down her legs as well.

She stood for a moment as the cool morning air touched her skin. Completely, for the first time in longer than she could remember. Had she ever stood naked in this room? Truly, she could not recall a single time. Dressing was a ritual of one garment being removed and then another going on. There wasn't a time that she didn't have at least a pair of stockings on.

Moving across the wooden floor, she looked at the full-length dressing mirror. Nervousness twisted her stomach and it also tightened her resolve. Why shouldn't she look at her own body? How could it be wicked? Anger flared to life as she straightened her back and moved closer to the reflection. Lynette took her first look at her body as the horizon began to turn pink.

Was she pretty? Or plain? She had no earthly way of knowing. The mirror displayed a body that was everything fashion despised but it looked rather correct to her eyes. Her breasts were twin globes of flesh that hung like teardrops and her nipples were little rose buttons. Her waist was trim but not as tiny as her corset made it.

Her mons looked soft and the memory of Sanders sucking on that little bud hidden within those folds made her blood pulse. The little bud gave a jerk as her passage ached for another touch from the stable master's finger.

Did a cock truly feel better? Lynette turned to look at the bed and couldn't recall her husband's cock feeling even good.

But she had not been hot.

The walls of her passage actually tingled as fluid moved down them. Lynette reached for her mons and felt the smooth slide of her own juices on her fingertips.

Returning to her discarded clothing, Lynette struggled back into them. The room brightened with the approach of day and her heated ideas felt more suited to the darkness.

But a little smile lifted her lips as she pushed the bolt open. Lady Celeste's invitation offered her more interesting company than her mother's current list of social regimens.

Now all she had to do was escape from her mother's virulent company.

* * * * *

"Will you join me for tea, Mother?"

Her mother smiled perfectly, not too bright and not too small. All of her expressions were practiced in front of her mirror each morning. Lynette knew that because she had spent the very same amount of time schooling her face into pleasing pleasantness at her mother's direction.

"I would enjoy some tea, my dear." Her mother sat on one of the nearby sofas as a maid entered and dropped a curtsy.

"The Lady Celeste."

The maid's announcement made Lynette smile. Celeste carefully unpinned her afternoon hat before handing the straw bonnet to the maid.

"I see I am not late for tea."

"Quite on time."

Celeste held out her gloved hands for Lynette's mother to grasp before she offered a daring smile to Lynette. The expression was hidden as she turned and took her seat ever so precisely at the table. The maid immediately came forward to serve afternoon tea.

"Lynette dear. I have brought you my most personal invitation and I simply will not listen to refusal."

Her mother's eyes shot over to Celeste as she smiled sweetly at her. "Just a simple gathering at my home for our anniversary. My husband has invited every member of his wedding party and all but one of them is yet to marry." Celeste lifted her tea to her lips before she smiled sweetly once again at Lynette's mother. "Has Lynette ever met Nigel Spencer?"

Her mother's emotions broke through her practiced control. Lynette lifted her teacup to hide her own astonishment. Nigel Spencer was the best catch in three states and her mother had never dreamed of hooking the man into marriage with her. With the kind of money he was rumored to have, he could demand a bride with blue blood.

Yet she had spent endless moments in his arms. During her first season, Nigel Spencer had partnered her at every gala dance. Lynette still remembered the excitement of waiting to see if he would show up. The man was a bit of a rake and didn't follow the season like a true gentleman would have.

However, when there was a fortune attached to your name, certain things were overlooked by the matrons and finger pointers. Lynette had savored those moments when Nigel swept through the door and took her dance card. Her heart raced just a little fast as she indulged in the fantasy that he came to see her alone.

But her father had married her to his friend and that ended Nigel's appearances that season. She would never know if he had other reasons, just that the night her father announced her engagement was the very last time she danced or even set eyes on Nigel.

"Nigel Spencer stood at your wedding?" Her mother's voice was smooth and calm but her eyes were as sharp as a hawk's were when it eyed a plump mouse.

"Indeed, George and he attended university together with William Saddler." Celeste turned her eyes to Lynette. "Of course, I will understand, dear, if your heart just isn't ready to move on."

"My daughter has packed her mourning dresses away." Her mother smiled at Celeste and shot Lynette a quick look. "She has decided to move on with life."

"Delightful." Celeste cast a look at her mother. "I would adore your company however I fear it does conflict with Lady Annabelle's wedding. George simply forbid me to attend due to our anniversary."

Lynette lifted her teacup to hide her expression. Lady Annabelle's wedding was the opening gala of the season! Her mother would rather die than miss the event. But Celeste was very clever indeed. An anniversary was one of the few reasons she and her husband might avoid the event and Lynette could sidestep it because she was just now reentering society. Her pride reared its head as she considered the neat manner Celeste had of maneuvering her mother into doing what she wanted. A kindred friend was one thing but one who wanted another toy to play with was quite another. Lynette just wished she didn't like the lady so much. It would be much simpler to decide if she had little emotion attached to the issues.

Her mother, on the other hand, could not afford to recall her agreement to attend. That simply was not done. Her mother's eyes flickered over her as she battled the need to keep Lynette under her eye and the temptation to jump at Celeste's bait of dangling Lynette under Nigel Spencer's and William Saddler's undivided attention. After all, she did not want a grown daughter under her roof any too long. The finger pointers would have plenty to say about her lack of skill in catching another husband for Lynette.

"Oh, and Anna Gilmore will be there as well. She stood up with me."

Her mother's eyes brightened as she looked over her tea at Lynette. Oh certainly, she knew that look from her mother! Three ladies spending the week together was most proper. Two might be frowned upon but no one would dare breathe a word against Anna Gilmore — she did boast blue blood.

What an interesting game life was. Lynette sipped her tea and glanced at the maid waiting nearby. Right then, Heather looked like a perfect maid, but Lynette couldn't help but wonder if the girl had been back to the stable that morning. Yet was that so wrong? Celeste appeared as grace incarnate but there was that most interesting frank conversation of last evening to add to her angelic looks. Lynette couldn't help but wonder what color stockings were hiding under her skirt. Were they plain white cotton or sheer black with red satin garters?

Nothing was as it appeared. Inside her own body lay the seeds of some unknown force that drove her towards temptation. Lynette felt more alive then she ever had as she glanced between the occupants of the room once more.

"I should be delighted to join you, Celeste."

Lynette felt her blood accelerate. Who could have suspected there was anything exciting about their conversation? Yet it was there in the slant of Celeste's eyes and the gentle topic. The maids had no idea that they were not every inch the delicate ladies they looked. Her mother only saw what she wanted to—another chance for her daughter to marry well.

Well, it would seem that life's mysteries were much more interesting than its realities.

* * * * *

"Pleasant dreams, my lady."

Heather tucked the bed clothing to its proper place over her breasts before she dropped a curtsy. The maid's skirts swished as she quickly left her lady's chamber.

Lynette looked around the dark room and sat up. She didn't want to lie on her back like a stone effigy. Heavens no! Life was short enough! She could lie in state when she was stone-cold dead.

She would be insane before dawn. Lynette kicked her bedding as her body burned. In that moment she hated all of the rules that kept her from enjoying her flesh.

Lynette rolled over and glared at the moon. She could not leave the house. It was simply too dangerous. There were too many maids and under-maids who might see her.

Instead, she would lie in her bed and burn. The folds of her sex were already slick with her juices. Begging for even a simple touch to ease their need.

Lynette considered the pulse from her passage. Sanders had made her spend with just his mouth. But he'd touched her pussy too. She had never done so. A lady did not even think of the spot between her legs, and she certainly never touched it. In fact, her husband touched it as briefly as possible.

Well, that made her angry! The pleasure was intensely amazing when her pussy was sucked. Why was that wrong? A blush burned her cheeks. Well, with Sanders it was not encouraged because the man was not her husband but why had her mother told her to lie flat on her back as her husband serviced her?

Rolling onto her back, Lynette pulled her nightgown up her legs until she could spread them. It was dark in the chamber yet she made certain the coverlet was concealing her actions. Reaching down, she gently brushed her own body with her hand. Her skin sent out a ripple of pleasure as she let her fingers rest over her spread sex.

A small smile lifted her lips as she gently stroked her body. Pleasure shot out as she repeated the action. Memory surfaced, making Lynette search for the spot at the top of her sex that Sanders had applied his tongue to. Her fingers became drenched with her own fluid as she gently felt along the folds of flesh. Right at the top, she found it. A little raised button. Very much like her nipple.

Pleasure immediately shot into her pussy as her fingers flicked over the little nub. Her skin turned hot as Lynette listened to the throb of her heartbeat in her ears. She moved her finger in a circle around and over the spot. Her hips began to twitch as everything twisted tighter and tighter with her touch.

Her body became desperate for relief. Tiny pants escaped her lips as she pressed and rubbed the slit between her thighs. The channel of her pussy begged to be stretched but Lynette kept her fingers moving over the little nub at the top of her sex.

Pleasure ripped into her belly as a moan left her mouth. Lynette let her hand rest on her bare belly as she felt each ripple of sensation travel through her body. It wasn't the intense release that Sanders had wrung from her, but it fed the hunger that lying in her cold bed wouldn't.

Perhaps she was wicked. Satisfaction moved over her body in little ripples and Lynette sighed. It was the honest truth that she did not care. It was her body and if she ever walked up an aisle to wed another man, her marriage would not be a cold one. Dealing with her hunger alone she could stomach. Lying beneath a man who instructed her to pray while he fucked, she could not!

Chapter Three

ഔ

"Lynette darling! I am so delighted you came!"

Celeste stood at the top of the home's entry steps as Lynette descended from her carriage. Another lady stood beside Celeste. Lady Anna Gilmore was quite connected in society. Lynette had only met the lady briefly, yet she knew her face very well. Indeed, her mother had made certain Lynette knew who all the important ladies were. Even if she couldn't quite manage a introduction.

"Hello, Lynette." Lynette dropped a curtsy as Lady Anna greeted her. The woman was her better and even claimed royal blood in her lineage.

"Now we shall not stand on formality while in the country." Lady Anna swept inside the house as Celeste and Lynette followed her. Anna sent Lynette a playful smile. "Celeste has told me what a dear friend you are and I must admit I am envious. So you must become my friend as well."

Lynette was swept along with the two ladies like a sister. Her lips lifted into a smile as she joined their banter and indulged herself in being part of such esteemed company. Yet her blood pulsed through her veins a little too fast. Was she being foolish to expect more from this gathering?

"I must change for dinner." Anna offered a kind smile before she turned and climbed the stairs. Lynette turned to find Celeste considering her with a serious face.

"Let's take a turn in the garden, Lynette."

They left the house behind as Celeste made odd comments about the flowers. Lynette swallowed her amusement because such remarks were the normal expectations of any lady. Before catching Sanders at his workbench she would not have considered them odd.

Wasn't it interesting the way a single moment could change a person's view? But her eyes were open and Lynette couldn't be content to seal out what she had seen. The reason was simple, it was not horrifying. Her body had twisted with delight and she wanted more of it. That or never to marry again. She should rather be alone with her knowledge than lying on her back as a husband serviced her like a cow. She could sit sedately in a rocking chair when her hair had gone completely white.

"Have you gone back to the stable?"

Lynette missed a step and Celeste smiled at her. "You don't look as if you did."

"Could you really see such a thing?" The words came out of her mouth and Lynette didn't attempt to halt them. There was no one about to judge them. Clearly, Celeste had taken her away from the ears of the house staff.

"Maybe." Celeste considered Lynette. "Your eyes look hungry, my dear. You must learn to hide that when others are with us. Too many simply do not understand." She walked in a little circle with her bustle trailing behind her before facing Lynette again. "I am rather relieved you didn't go back to the stable. The staff talk too much and you must be very careful, my dear."

"I believe that is why I didn't go." Lynette felt her curiosity rise past her caution. "Why did you invite me?"

Celeste grabbed her hand and took her down the garden path. "Look, Lynette! No one about for miles! We only have to hide from the staff." Celeste turned and hugged her. "It is very simple, you will swear you stood by my side and I will declare you never left my sight! So simple and you may have the freedom to do whatever you wish! Anything, Lynette, indulge your flesh here because I could never scold you for something that I feel myself." She spun in another circle before stopping with her hands over her heart. "I have needs, Lynette…for my husband."

Lynette smiled and then giggled. Celeste lost her tense look as she lifted an eyebrow at her amusement. Lynette sobered long enough to aim a stern look that her mother would have envied at Celeste. "How unfashionable."

"Don't be hateful, Lynette. It is my anniversary. I made an honest man of him after all."

Indeed it was and Lynette envied Celeste the excitement sparkling in her eyes. How amazing it must be to feel life jumping all around you. She had always been taught to cherish calmness but the truth was she craved that pulsing tempo that had sent her into pleasure on a stable workbench.

Yes, Lynette envied Celeste because the lady held something even more remarkable than pleasure. She loved her husband and the sparkle lighting her eyes was fueled by that tender emotion. She didn't leave her marriage bed wondering and seeking more. In fact, she was concocting ways to spend more time in that very bed.

Her mother would have fainted dead away.

"George would like a child and I must see to that after this weekend."

Lynette was suddenly confused. She would have thought that Celeste's need would help a great deal in the conception of children.

"Come Lynette, we must have tea." Celeste took her down the path too quickly, but her heart accelerated and Lynette savored the moment as life became exciting just because they were playing.

It had been ever so long since she had played!

Celeste had tea served and Anna sat for a cup as well. Lynette sipped at the dark brew but found it hard to swallow.

"Drink it, Lynette. This brew is quite helpful in keeping the waist slim." Celeste looked over her cup as Lynette took a larger swallow. Celeste smiled as she sat her empty cup aside. "I shall have no more of it after this weekend."

Anna turned her head to look at Celeste. "Time for a family, dear?"

Celeste nodded as Anna smiled and finished her tea. Lynette looked at the dark concoction and sealed herself to finish her own cup.

A man entered the doorway but it wasn't the butler. His eyes swept the room and stopped on Lynette. A frown darkened his face as he continued to study her.

"Nigel! You rogue! I am surprised I even recognize you because it has been forever since you showed that face in my home." Celeste added a pretty pout to her words and Nigel turned his attention to her. He swept his hat off and executed a perfect bow, the man even clicked his heels as he did it.

"Celeste, dear lady, wherever is George? I will be delighted to call him out for leaving you with any time to think about other men."

"Oh stop, Nigel." Celeste fluttered her eyelashes as Nigel brushed her gloved hand with his lips. It wasn't quite the light kiss that Lynette was accustomed to getting from gentlemen. This was a lingering contact of lips to gloved hand and Celeste held her breath as she watched. Nigel straightened and offered her a smile as he released her hand. Celeste smiled like a little girl who had just wandered into the kitchen as the cook was baking teacakes.

"Do you know Lynette Edwardmoore? She's been away for mourning but is joining the season."

Those sharp eyes returned to her face as Nigel considered her. "My sympathies. Your parents?"

"Her husband." Celeste moved back into the parlor as the butler took Nigel's hat and coat. "I have rescued her from her mother's plans to dangle her in front of all of Lady Annabelle's wedding guests."

"A debt we share." Nigel moved in front of her and reached for her hand. Lynette was frozen in place as he loomed over her. The man's eyes looked far too knowing as they moved over her face. She couldn't remember another man ever looking at her quite that intensely before.

Celeste pinched her and Lynette jumped. Nigel's lips twitched at the corners as she placed her hand into his. He closed his hand and her heart accelerated. It was a silly reaction but Lynette couldn't quite blame it on any one thing. Nigel's eyes sank into hers before he lowered his head to kiss her hand.

Her heart jumped again and this time Lynette frowned. Her gloved hand had been kissed countless times since her début season. She forced her lips back into their calm smile as Nigel lifted those sharp eyes back to hers. The man appeared to enjoy watching her.

Lynette pulled her hand from his but his fingers didn't release hers. Instead he let her go slowly as his fingers slipped down the length of hers. It was a soft touch that sent a shiver up her arm. His lips twitched up as though he knew exactly what the touch did to her.

"Nigel, stop frightening Lynette." George appeared in the parlor doorframe and Nigel laughed before turning to clasp hands with his friend. Nigel turned his eyes back to her and raised a dark eyebrow.

"I don't believe she is frightened or even offended. In fact, I detect a hint of amusement in those blue eyes."

George sent her a grin as Nigel took Lady Anna's gloved hand. The maid entered the room with fresh tea as Lynette tried to keep her body from moving. Her blood was moving so quickly through her veins, remaining on the brocade-covered sofa was near impossible. Her brain insisted on picking up little hints of something...forbidden in the conversation that flowed around her. Celeste had always struck her that way but now she was the only one who didn't offer dark promises with her eyes as the sugar bowl passed about.

The second tea was quite normal, not the bitter concoction that had been served first. Lynette raised her eyes from her cup to catch Nigel watching her. The man's eyes were...well...arrogant. They moved over her hair and down her body without a care that anyone might notice. Lynette had a suspicion that he enjoyed her notice of it. It was a sort of dare. A test of her composure and a playful inducement to return the looks.

Countless hours in front of her dressing table mirror had taught her iron control of her face and Lynette smiled sweetly back at Nigel before she let her eyes slip over his shoulders. The man was large and his chest broad. He wasn't sitting but leaned against the doorframe, and that allowed her to move down his frame and even over the front of his trousers. That little shiver ran through her again as she considered what he had in those trousers. The fabric didn't give her even a hint of what size cock he had and that sent a small wave of disappointment through her.

Lynette scolded her curiosity and jerked her eyes back up his body only to have her breath freeze in her lungs as she found Nigel watching her. All amusement had vanished. Nigel's eyes considered her with blatant interest that would have shocked her a mere month ago. Today it made her blood heat as she looked straight back into his dark eyes.

Lynette enjoyed it.

* * * * *

Celeste certainly did intend to deceive the rest of society. Lynette found herself alone as dinner was cleared away. A little tune filled her thoughts as she gave in to the urge to hum quietly. The evening was gently giving way to night as she strolled towards the labyrinth.

The grounds on the estate were delightful and the labyrinth tall and large. Most older estates had a maze contrasted with hedges. Lynette had often played in her parents' labyrinth with her governess on many a summer morning.

As she entered the labyrinth, the scent of jasmine filled her head and she smiled as the tune slipped away. Who cared that the night was wasted on a simple stroll? Life moved through her body as it had never done so before. Perhaps that was contentment. Lynette smiled – it felt more like happiness and she had missed the feeling. She strolled deeper into the maze as her eyes adjusted to the dark. Excitement warmed her cheeks as she indulged in the rare opportunity to be out in the dark.

A deep groan filtered through the shrubs as Lynette halted. Walls of greenery met her eyes but another deep groan came from somewhere deeper in the maze. The sound didn't alarm her, quite the opposite. It sent a zip of excitement through her that went all the way to her clit because she recognized the sound on that same forbidden level that had sent her deeper into the stables.

It was a groan of male pleasure.

"Enough, Celeste, I want to fuck you." A husky female giggle drifted through the greenery as the rustle of satin taffeta hit her ear. Lynette smiled as she recalled the dress Celeste had worn to dinner. She had no idea how the couple intended to fuck in the labyrinth. Didn't Celeste need to be on her back for that?

"God, George, I love your cock." There was another rustle of taffeta and then a series of wet sounds. Another hard grunt and more wet sounds and Lynette turned back the way she came. Heat pooled in her belly as an odd jealousy engulfed her.

Her body throbbed with need as she lingered over her retreat. Right or wrong, she wanted the same thing that Celeste was getting. She wanted to know what it felt like to be fucked, when you wanted to be fucked. Not lying beneath a husband who reminded you to be still while he plowed you like a cornfield.

Celeste certainly liked her husband's cock inside her body. Lynette moved further away as she felt her pussy heat with just the idea. Paul's cock had always hurt her and she had lain still in an effort to see the duty done quickly.

But she had never been wet. Lynette felt fluid on the top of her thighs as she walked, and considered the fact that her pussy was spilling that fluid. Was that the difference? Sanders had asked her if she was wet and she was. She wove through the labyrinth until the sounds of the couple faded.

"They sound like they are having more fun than we are."

Lynette gasped and stared into Nigel's sharp eyes. He was waiting around a bend in the maze where a bench was placed for resting while navigating the large labyrinth. Curiosity filled those dark eyes right then as he considered her reaction to his comment. One eyebrow rose as Lynette felt a little heat fill her cheeks.

"They are married."

"So they are. They even appear to be enjoying it." Nigel considered her once again and let his eyes slip down her body. It was more than bold but Lynette didn't find it insulting. Instead, she enjoyed the fact that a man like Nigel was interested in looking at her. Heat moved through her veins, warming her body beneath her dress in response.

"I am most pleasantly surprised, Lynette." Nigel's eyes found hers again as his mouth pressed into a firm line. Her stomach gave an odd twist of excitement as he dropped his eyes to her lips. "I am very surprised indeed. However did you manage to fool Paul Edwardmoore into thinking you were an innocent?"

"Because I was." Lynette frowned at him. Nigel smiled at her gently before his hand snaked forward to capture hers. The contact was jarring. Heat raced up her arm and into her chest where her nipples reacted by tightening beneath her corset.

"Forgive me, that was the wrong word. I should have suggested that you fooled the man into thinking you were a cold fish." His fingers stroked her palm before his thumb moved the top of her glove aside and found the sensitive skin of her inner wrist. Lynette gasped again because pleasure shot up her arm from the contact. It was skin to skin because Nigel wasn't wearing gloves. His eyes watched her face the entire time and his face showed his satisfaction. It deepened her enjoyment to know he savored the touch as well.

It was an odd emotion to feel but Lynette liked the way Nigel was looking at her. Hunger chewed at her body as his eyes witnessed the blush burning her checks.

She wasn't frightened of him or even herself, and Nigel found it spellbinding. In a world that shunned the most basic instincts of a man and woman, Lynette was a rare creature. She was also a delightful one. The little naughty smile she'd worn as she came around the corner made him chuckle. Inside the polished exterior was a woman that he felt drawn to. He didn't need a porcelain doll for a wife. What he craved was a woman who could match him when the bed curtains were drawn.

"I am going to court you, Lynette."

She pulled her hand but Nigel held it firmly in his grip. Lynette's eye's rounded slightly at his audacity but he moved his thumb over her wrist again and those eyes brightened with pleasure too.

"I am not certain I wish to be courted."

"Should I ask your father?"

She jerked her hand away and Nigel let it go before he hurt her. Anger glowed in her eyes and she didn't much care if he saw it. She was never going to marry another man who viewed her as chattel. "That will do you no good. My parents might want me to marry but I do not have to, sir!"

He laughed at her temper. Lynette turned away but gasped as a hard arm slid around her waist. The hard length of Nigel pressed against her side as his warm scent filled her head. She actually enjoyed the way he smelled, it went into her lungs and set off another throb in her clit. Nigel held her against his body and her side felt the unmistakable shape of his hard cock.

"I'm delighted to hear that you've become your own woman, Lynette." His lips were a mere inch from her ear and she shivered as he leaned down and laid a soft kiss on her neck. Pleasure shot into her pussy. It was a blunt sensation that made her jerk against his arm. There was just so much sensation that her body convulsed before her brain formed a single thought.

"Relax." His other hand found the side of her face and turned her to look into his eyes again. Determination blazed from them making her breath lodge in her throat. "I want to taste you before you run away."

"I was angry, not frightened." And Lynette needed to make sure he knew that. "I respect my father but I will not blindly obey him again."

His eyes dropped to her lips and her mouth went dry. "Then I will make sure you dream of me tonight, Lynette." His mouth captured hers as his hand held her face in place. His lips moved over hers with firm demand as a little whimper of delight escaped her throat

Nigel pressed her mouth open further and his tongue swept inside. His hand turned her head as he stroked her tongue with his, tempting her to join the wild kiss. Pleasure and excitement pulsed through her and she refused to miss the chance to deepen the sensations. Her tongue stroked his as a groan emerged from his throat.

It was pure madness and Lynette savored it! Nigel moved his lips over her cheek and onto her neck. His hand cradled her face as he laid a line of hard kisses down the column of her throat. The throbbing in her clit doubled as he turned her to face him.

A soft pop hit her ears as the first button on her collar opened. Nigel's lips found the newly bared flesh and licked it. Lynette shivered but her hands lifted and found his shoulders as another button popped open. Surrounded by moonlight and shrubs, it would be so simple to indulge her whims.

As easily as she had given way to the suggestions of a stable master.

Yet this was different. Lynette let her fingers wander over the firm set of shoulders as another of her buttons yielded to Nigel's fingers. His lips left her neck as his eyes found hers. The tips of his fingers brushed the swells of her breast and all Lynette did was mutter with delight.

Pleasure flowed down her body and her nipples pushed against the restriction of her corset in a bid for freedom. They were tightened into hard buttons that she had never known could feel so acutely. At that moment, the idea of Nigel applying his lips to them almost buckled her knees.

Nigel threw his head back and laughed. "Forget the courtship, Lynette, I want to move on to the wedding night."

"So I gather." The words might have sounded more proper if Lynette could have held her amusement from bubbling out right after them. Nigel shifted and her thigh suddenly told her exactly what was on his mind — the man's cock was hard and pressed through the layers of clothing between them. Nigel's hand moved her face until their eyes met again. Simple enjoyment shimmered back at her and Lynette didn't try to contain her smile. Naughty or even wicked, that did not bother her. She was enjoying the embrace and had no intention of saying she did not.

"You are a rare treasure, Lynette. I should warn you that I meant exactly what I said." His eyes dropped to the open bodice as hunger replaced that enjoyment. Her breath froze in place as her pussy twisted with need.

"Why do you warn me?" Her fingers itched to drop to that hard erection. Hunger gnawed at her body, making it impossible to think about why she should not let her hand trace the outline of his cock.

"Because most ladies do not handle lust well." His hand moved from her waist to her hip and pressed her against his body. "But love always gets its roots from that darker emotion. I'm not interested in playing a child's courting game. You should run away if you don't want to discover how a man courts a woman."

His hands released her and her body protested the loss of contact. Hunger twisted through her and so did need. The idea of joining Lady Annabelle's wedding made her cringe. Right here there was only a man and a woman. Excitement surged through her as well as a feeling of confidence. Nigel wanted to drop their facades, and it answered her longings.

Lynette smiled into the sharp eyes watching her as she let her needs rise above her endless lessons on propriety. Surrounded by moonlight, those ideas were foreign and unpractical. Her hand raised and she placed it over that tempting cock. Nigel's face tightened as his breath hissed softly. Lynette smoothed her fingers over the rigid length. "I am most interested in how a man pays court to a woman."

His cock wanted to explode. Nigel tightened his control as her fingers smoothed over his erection. The swells of her breasts tempted him to seek out her nipples but her fingers tore him with indecision.

Her face wasn't clouded with images of hooking a good catch. Marriage wasn't something he sought because it was always some game of name and money. There were times he envied the common men working his estate because they could marry a woman who loved them for themselves. Her fingers moved to the opening of his pants and Nigel grinned. He brushed them aside as he opened his pants for her.

"Have you ever handled a cock?"

Her eyelashes fluttered as indecision crossed her face for the first time. Nigel raised her face back to his as he searched her eyes. "Tell me, Lynette."

His voice was firm. Lynette felt nervousness flood her. Should she tell him about Sanders? It might bring the evening to an abrupt halt. Lynette straightened her back. If Nigel did leave because of her morning with Sanders...then she didn't want him. "Yes."

A smile appeared on his face as he caught one of her hands and placed it on his freed cock. Lynette gasped as she felt the hard length against her palm. Her pussy sent out a wail of need that made her shake.

"Do you have a lover?" Nigel sounded jealous.

"No. I did not let him have me."

The cock in her hand throbbed as she let her fingers wandered over its head. A drop of fluid hit her skin as she curled her fingers around the width and moved her hand back down towards the base.

"I found one of my maids in the stable. After she left, the stable master caught me looking at his cock." Her fingers moved over the head of his cock again. "It was the first time I'd ever met a man willing to let me look at his erection."

"But you didn't let him fuck you?" Nigel's hand left her face to stroke the exposed swells of her breasts. "Would you let me?"

"I don't know." And truthfully she didn't. All hints of playfulness were gone and Nigel was once again looking at her with sharp eyes. She felt almost like a sweet that he wanted to pop into his mouth. A shiver shook her body as she thought about Nigel feasting on her spread body. The intensity of it would be enough to shatter her sanity. The cock in her hand suddenly filled her with a wicked idea. She looked at the length in her hand and then back up at Nigel.

"Do women taste men's genitals?"

Nigel's face clouded with anger. "You will never let that man suck you off again, Lynette."

He sounded jealous and Nigel didn't care! The sweet smell of her pussy drifted to his nose and all that filled him was the fact that she was hot for him. "I will make you forget all about his efforts. Put your foot up on the bench."

His voice was commanding and it tightened the excitement racing through her. If she raised her foot and did as he said her thighs would be spread. She might never have thought of such a thing before but her body hummed with approval of doing it.

Lynette lifted her foot and Nigel grunted. It was a harsh male sound of approval but one that made her body pulse with even greater need. She liked this dark, rough manner. There was a hint of savage tendency that made it even more intense.

"God, your pussy smells good." His hand swept her skirt up and over her thigh. Lynette gasped as the night air brushed her spread body. Nigel lowered his frame to one knee as his eyes focused on her thigh. He smoothed his hand over her leg and right to the spread lips of her sex. The tip of one finger slipped through her wet folds as she shivered.

"No drawers, my dear? I'm most pleasantly shocked." He smoothed a hand over her bare thigh once again. "Do not move, Lynette."

She didn't want to. Nigel stroked his way to her spread body and ran his fingers the length of her slit and then once again before he thrust that finger up into her. A little whimper came from her as she felt the walls of her passage try to grip his finger. She felt so empty...so needy for what she had only dreamed of having. Nigel grunted again as he pulled his finger free. His eyes raised to hers as he moved his hands to her bottom. "Your pussy was made for me, Lynette."

It was an odd comment but it made her tremble. Nigel watched her face as she contemplated his words. His hand stroked her inner thigh as he stared up into her eyes. "I will enjoy proving that to you."

His hands captured her bottom as he leaned forward. A cry escaped her throat as his breath hit her spread sex. One of his hands spread apart the folds shielding her pussy before the tip of his tongue found her. Pleasure roared through her as he lapped the center of her slit...once...twice and then again. She ached so badly she whimpered with the need. Nigel laughed softly as he found her clit and sucked the throbbing bud into his mouth.

Her head fell back as her body convulsed. Her hips thrust forward as he sucked on her and her hands grasped his shoulders as a climax taunted her. Coming over his mouth wouldn't be enough. She knew that now. She wanted the cock her hand had touched so briefly. She craved it thrusting into her body, filling her until she screamed with release.

Nigel thrust one thick finger up into her body as his tongue lapped over her clit. Her passage tried to grasp that digit before he withdrew it and thrust it up into her again. She was balanced on the edge of climax, so close to release but never getting close enough to be carried away by it.

"Ah Lynette, your pussy is sweet. I could spend an hour just tasting it. Licking my way to your clit and then back down to your pussy."

Oh God! She couldn't survive an hour of his teasing! A moan came from her chest as her hips thrust up to offer her clit to his mouth. A low rumble of laughter hit her ears a second before Nigel sucked even harder on her clit as he thrust two fingers up into her pussy. She cried out as pleasure ripped her in two. Her blood raced so fast her head spun but her hips jerked and pressed towards Nigel's mouth as he sucked until she sighed with relief.

"And that, my dear, is only the beginning of what my wife would be expected to endure in my bed."

A little giggle escaped her mouth because his words sounded so very proper and their position was so completely improper! Nigel stood up but stroked her slit with a single finger as his eyes watched hers. He found her bud with the tip of that finger and rubbed it gently.

"Suck my cock." His words were firm and they shocked her a bit. His fingertip moved on her clit again as he caught her chin with his other hand. His eyes burned into hers as he rubbed her slit again. "Drop to your knees and lick the length of my cock."

It was so simple to obey him, after all, she had been reared to obey the males in her family. This was different though. It was naughty, wicked, possibly immoral, but excitement raced through her as she let her eyes drop to the hard cock in question. The ruby head and thick staff promised her an end to her need to be stretched as she came.

"I won't fuck you until you wrap those sweet lips around my cock."

It was an odd threat but one that worked. Her body wasn't satisfied, not by half. Nigel rubbed and teased her clit, awakening it again, and this time nothing was going to soothe her but a thick cock. She instinctively knew that. The image of Heather being fucked and liking it played through her mind as she wrapped her fingers around Nigel's cock.

A little hum of appreciation came from his chest as she lowered her foot from the bench and then knelt at his feet. Closing her fingers around the staff, Lynette stroked the whole length of the rod and then over the head. There was a slit on its crown and a drop of fluid sitting in it. Lynette rubbed that fluid away as she moved her hand back down his cock to its base.

Being on her knees should have felt submissive but instead she was enthralled by the idea of making Nigel as frantic as she had been. Could a woman bring a man to climax with her mouth? Lynette looked at the ruby head of Nigel's cock and decided she was going to find out!

"Ah yes, that's it."

Lynette smiled around his cock before she relaxed her jaw and opened her mouth wider. His hips pushed the organ towards her face as she used her fingers to stroke the part of it that she couldn't get into her mouth. A mutter of male enjoyment came from Nigel as Lynette used her tongue to stroke the slit.

Slipping her hands down the length, she cupped the twin sacs hanging at the base. A deep groan was her reward as his hips thrust towards her face. It was amazing how much she enjoyed hearing his groans of pleasure. Lynette sucked on his cock as her hand stroked and tightened on the rod and the sound of his pleasure prompted her to take even more of his cock into her mouth. Nigel's hand was fisted in her hair and suddenly he pulled her mouth away from his cock.

"Enough!" His voice was harsh as he looked at her with blazing eyes. "I am going to fuck you, Lynette."

She gasped as Nigel tightened his grip on her hair and bent his knees until they were staring into each other's eyes. "Right here, right now, I am going to let you feel what my cock is like inside your sweet pussy." He stood up and took her with him. He held onto her hair as his eyes watched her and his other hand found her knee and lifted it to set her foot on the bench once again.

"Put my cock into your pussy, Lynette."

"What?" She had never heard such a thing. Well, there were a great number of things happening at that moment that were quite the revelation but could a woman actually be the one in the lead?

"Grasp my cock and fit it into your slit. Show me what you crave."

She shivered as her hand reached for his length. She did crave it. This carnal pleasure. Her pussy was so empty it ached. Her fingers found his hot rod and curved around it. His eyes bore into hers as she guided it to the wet opening to her pussy.

His hand clasped her bottom and tilted her hips up as the head of his cock stretched her body. "Ah Lynette, I am going to teach you what this pussy was created for."

His hips thrust forward as his hand held her bottom in place. That hard cock split open her tight sheath as she gasped. Her body burned around his invasion but pleasure still made her hips twitch up towards his, offering her body to the hard thrust of his. His hands lifted her right off the ground as he straightened to his full height. Lynette grasped his shoulders to keep her body from falling away from his. His hips bucked and sent his cock deeper into her pussy.

"Oh yes, Nigel. I've longed for this."

He laughed, but not at her. Instead it was a manner of sharing between them. They were both addicts, feeding off each other. He pulled free of her body and then thrust up into her deeper. Little wet sounds came from her body as he began to move. Deep thrusts that made her whimper with delight.

Lynette wanted it to last forever! Her body was a churning mass of pleasure that all centered around the hard cock thrusting into her. He filled her and stretched her and most importantly, fed her need to be fucked!

No wonder Heather snuck off to the stable. The labyrinth was now a place that she would gladly scamper off to as long as there was a lover waiting to join her in moonlight-inspired madness.

Climax jerked her into its hold as Nigel groaned and thrust faster between her thighs. His hands tightened on her bottom as his hips drove his cock up into her body. A hot spurt of fluid hit the deepest part of her pussy and her muscles clenched around his cock. Lynette's eyes flew open to find Nigel's burning into them as his cock twitched inside her.

The warm smell of his skin filled her senses and she still couldn't muster any true regret. Her body drifted on waves of satisfaction as Nigel placed a warm kiss on her lips. He lingered over her mouth, slowly tasting and stroking her tongue with his.

"Ah, sweet Lynette, dream of me and the bed we will share as husband and wife." Nigel lowered her feet back to the ground as he slipped from her body. His warm palm cupped her cheek. "Tell me you will marry me."

His words sounded more like an order. Her skirts fell back into place but her thighs were slick, making for an odd combination of proper and hidden dishevelment. A naughty smile played across her lips as she swept past the bench.

"I know so little about you, sir."

His eyes flashed with renewed lust and something a little deeper that almost frightened her. Nigel wasn't playing any game designed to get between her thighs for a quick moment of stolen sin. No, possession lit his eyes and he aimed that strong male emotion right at her. "I will enjoy every moment of making certain that you know me intimately, Lynette."

She shivered in response. Finding herself the target of Nigel's interest unleashed powerful emotions that sent her walking towards the manner house. She heard his deep chuckle but Nigel didn't follow her. Lynette was grateful for the privacy.

Her body still pulsed with delight as her brain began to twist Nigel's marriage proposal around. Proposal? Not quite that. The man was giving her an order that he expected to be obeyed.

That was not uncommon in husbands. Her lips turned back up into a naughty smile as she considered how much more satisfying Nigel's orders were as far as wifely duties. She might just be able to adjust to his...ideas.

Oh, she was naughty! The ideas that swirled through her head were born from temptation. Well, that didn't banish them or the pulse that her blood carried to her pussy. She couldn't detest her own body. In fact, she didn't want to.

Lynette climbed the stairs to her room and sighed as she found a tub waiting in her chamber. Two housemaids followed her from the main floor and she was grateful for the excuse to unlace all her layers of clothing.

The question of Nigel Spencer could wait until she enjoyed her bath. She smiled as the maid untied the top knot on her corset. Indeed, she might just enjoy making the man prove himself.

Chapter Four

ॐ

"So, Lynette, are you going to marry me?"

Two plates dropped from the maid's fingers as Lynette fumbled her fork on the fine china. She glared at Nigel as he lounged in the doorframe. He shot her a grin that betrayed the little boy still lurking inside his personality, before he looked at Celeste.

"Did Lynette tell you that I laid my name at her feet and she most cruelly made me wait all night long?"

"Stop, Nigel." A giggle ruined the effect of her words.

"Whatever for, Lynette?" Nigel moved into the room and pulled her chair back. A second later he scooped her up and twirled her across the patio floor. Her skirts flared out as she went and another giggle floated along with her petticoat ruffle. A moment later her feet touched the floor again.

"I've never proposed to a lady before so you must forgive me if I bungle it a bit. Your father married you off far too quickly, while I was distracted by courting you." His hand grasped hers and pulled her around in a wide circle like children did when they played. It had been forever since she played!

"You jest, sir!"

"Not so!" Nigel caught her waist and lifted her off the floor as he spun in a tight circle that made her stomach clench tight. "I was dancing with you under the watchful eyes of too many ample-bosomed chaperones, while Paul was courting your father."

That was true. Lynette looked at the face that had turned her around a dance floor in her first season. There had been moments when she allowed her young heart to play with loving him but her practical brain always intruded, helped along by her parents who made sure to appear before the last note died away.

It might be simple to believe that Nigel harbored tender feelings for her but her brain wondered just why he was only bringing them to light now. Was it because she had yielded her body to his? If so, that certainly contradicted everything she had ever been taught about catching a man like him.

"Come riding with me, Lynette. I want to work my devilish charms on you before your father finds some insensitive fool to try and marry you to."

Celeste laughed from her spot at the patio table. She blew Lynette a kiss as she fluttered her eyelashes. "Go on, you two, before you knock over any more of my china."

Nigel offered her a bow before he captured Lynette's hand and strode from the room. It was a high-handed gesture, just taking her away like that. But a wave of excitement hit her belly as she hurried behind his large shoulders.

Work his charms on her? Well, she did confess to a fair bit of anticipation for that!

Her morning dress didn't have a bustle because she had intended to change into her riding habit as soon as the meal was finished. At home she didn't even bother to dine in the morning, her maid brought her a simple tray. Her mother fully approved because light eating kept her waist tiny. All that much better for catching a husband.

Lynette was sick unto death of needing to attract a marriage offer.

"Do you like to ride?"

Nigel looked over his shoulder as he continued on to the stable.

"Yes, in truth, I ride every morning."

A promise flickered across his face as they rounded the stable corner and Lynette saw that Nigel had already had two mounts saddled for them. Excitement fluttered in her belly again as she noted the two horses...just two.

The morning air was crisp as Nigel set out and her mare followed. Lynette laughed as he set a fast pace and flashed her a grin as she followed suit. She leaned over the neck of her mare and kept her bottom firmly in the side-saddle.

"I have a surprise for you, Lynette." The grin was gone and in its place was a hard expression of determination. Passion flickered in his eyes once again as Nigel turned them towards the forest. All hints of the boy were gone now. Lynette stared at a man.

Her blood heated in response. Nigel led her deeper into the forest as she felt the last bits of society's controls dissipate behind them, as they wove through the trees. Details of their lives peeled away until it was just the two of them there, one man, one woman and the fire that nature bred in them both.

"There it is." Nigel urged his mount forward as the woods revealed a small house. "George's hunting lodge."

Most estates had them. These lodges were secret places where the men stole off to when they were hunting or, as her mother had often whispered, meeting their mistresses.

A lady ignored the presence of such places on her own estate. Paul had one and Lynette suddenly wondered if he had met a woman there. It was an odd idea to think that the man who had instructed her to lie still while he mated her might have gone into the woods to meet a woman willing to suck his cock.

Nigel swung his leg over his mount and reached for her waist. He lowered her to the ground just a bare inch from his body and she caught that warm male scent of his skin. His eyes burned into hers as he stroked one of her cheeks. "Would you like to go inside with me, Lynette?"

He was testing her. Seeing just how she might react to the idea of being alone with him again. Dark memories of last night filled her brain as she felt her clit pulse to life with a little throb of need.

A deep chuckle rumbled from his throat before he leaned down and kissed her. It was a deep kiss that thrust into her mouth, filling her just like his cock had last night. It was a little sample of the decadence that she craved and Lynette sent her own tongue to mingle with his.

Nigel pulled his mouth from hers and groaned. "You are going to marry me, Lynette."

She stepped away from the arrogance of that statement. "I am not so certain I will." Turning back to stare at him, she lifted one eyebrow. "I am enjoying being free to make my own decisions."

His face darkened but she didn't fear his displeasure. Instead she held her head high and stared right back into his angry eyes. "You have not once professed any affection for me. I will not be a possession again."

One corner of his mouth lifted slightly. He gathered the reins of her mare and twisted them around his gloved hand. "No, you will be my wife. I want a woman in my bed, Lynette, not some frightened child. You've grown up quite nicely and I am going to enjoy helping you finish that process."

He flashed her a hard promise before he led her mare and his horse to a small stable just next to the lodge. Her stomach knotted as she realized he was putting the horses out of sight because he intended to be there for a good amount of time.

A shiver shook her as she considered just what he might do with her in unlimited time. Nigel returned and held out his hand. His eyes dared her to lay her palm against his as one of his dark eyebrows rose in question. "Frightened? Quite possibly you should be. I have no intentions of being a gentleman."

Her blood surged forward as her hand landed in his. "That does not mean I intend to marry you." Lynette had no idea where her boldness came from. But she filled her chest and stared right back at Nigel and his displeasure.

"Then I shall just have to change your mind, Lynette. I'm going to enjoy it too."

He turned to the door and pulled her inside with him. Her mouth curved into a little smile as she noticed a large wicker basket on the table, and she caught just a hint of fresh baked bread coming from it. A bottle of wine sat neatly next to it. Apparently Nigel planned his seductions well.

Nigel pulled her behind him across the room and pushed open a door that led to a bedroom. The drapes were all closed, making it dark and strangely inviting with its large bed. He spun her around and let her go towards that bed. When she turned around, he was unfastening the buttons of his coat.

"I can't wait to get back inside you, Lynette. If those damn maids hadn't been helping you bathe, I would have fucked you again last night." The jacket was laid over a tapestry chair as he sat down and stretched his feet out.

"Take my boots off." He watched her to see what she made of his order. The idea that he meant to disrobe today made her body surge with heat. Last night had certainly been delightful but the idea of being completely bare was ten times more enticing. Skin to skin the sensations must be amazing.

"All right." She bent over and took one of his boots in her hands. It came free with a good jerk and Lynette sat it on the floor. She reached for the other one and sat it next to the first. Nigel stood up and stroked her cheek. "Good girl. But I confess, I would have enjoyed a reason to punish you."

"Punish? I thought you said you wanted a woman here with you, Nigel." His fingers were busy on his shirt and Lynette found her eyes following them as a thin patch of his chest was reveled. Dark hair curled through the opening of his shirt as Nigel laughed.

"Ah Lynette, a little discipline can be very stimulating." He shrugged his shirt off and her breath froze. His chest was magnificent. Covered in dark hair and packed with firm muscle. He just looked incredibly male to her. Her pussy heated in response, telling her that her body fully approved of this man being her lover.

"In fact there are many things that bring pleasure. I enjoy pleasure, Lynette. I have been searching for a woman who enjoys it as much as I do. Like Celeste does."

"I do enjoy it...with you." Nigel pulled his pants open and a little whimper caught in her throat. His cock was hard and swollen. Promising her another hard ride that her pussy begged for.

"I need more, Lynette." He laid his pants aside and stood there for her eyes to roam over. Stepping forward, he tipped her chin up so that their eyes met. "I need you to be free with me, free to explore what our bodies like. Free to leave society behind a closed door and just indulge who we are beneath our clothing and names."

It was so tempting! Like offering water to the desert traveler! She was parched, dying of thirst and Nigel offered her an oasis in a sea of burning sand.

"Take your clothes off, Lynette." His voice was soft but edged in steel. A flame of excitement shot up her spine as she obeyed him. Wicked little ideas spun to her, thoughts about things that he might order her to do. Submitting had never seemed so exciting before.

"Yes, Nigel." She purred the words and began to take her gloves off. She pulled on each fingertip before sliding the suede free. Her skin enjoyed the freedom and the rest of her body begged for the same. Nigel watched her with complete devotion. Although she was the one submitting, he was her slave at that moment. Each button that she opened on her bodice captured his attention.

The wind sent the branches of a tree against a windowpane as she laid her dress over a dresser. Her petticoat followed, leaving her in her corset and drawers. She was helpless then, the laces running down the back of the tight garment.

"God, Lynette, I have waited so damn long to find you." Nigel growled the words as he stood up and turned her away from him. His fingers found her laces and worked the top knot free. Her breasts instantly rejoiced as the first holes were unlaced, freeing them from their confinement.

Nigel tossed the corset away and turned her around. He reached for the tail of her thin chemise and pulled it over her head. His eyes dropped to her bared breasts and she stared in fascination at his face. She was beautiful in his eyes. The look simmering in those dark orbs said far more than a mirror might have told her.

She stepped out of her drawers and stood proudly before him. His eyes moved down her body, taking in every curve before returning to her face. "I will deny you nothing, Lynette, except the right to refuse me."

"Even a lover?" She smiled at her own jest as she trailed her fingers through the crisp hair on his chest. She couldn't resist the temptation to touch him any longer. The inches between them were as wide as yards.

His nostrils flared as he caught her hair and pulled the pins from it. "A lover, Lynette? You may have one if I can." His lips brushed her mouth as her hair tumbled free. "I could share you with another man. My cock in your pussy and his in your bottom."

She gasped but heat speared through her pussy. Nigel pressed another kiss onto her mouth as he looked into her eyes. "That excites you, doesn't it?" His hand cupped one of her breasts and gently squeezed. "It excites me too. Yet there is one restriction—you will never fuck another man unless I am there too."

What a forbidden thing. Two men and one woman? "You would marry a woman who did that?"

His eyebrow rose. "I would only marry a woman who understood my needs. I need to hear you cry with pleasure when I fuck you. I need to be a man when the doors are closed. I need you to say to hell with all of the rules that tell us what we can't do with our own bodies." His thumb brushed her nipple, making her moan. "Sharing you would be far too much fun to miss out on. Would you watch as I fucked another woman? I will never go to another bed, my sweet, but I will bring any mistress to our bed to share with you."

His mouth caught hers in a hard kiss of ownership. His hand held her head in place as he pushed her mouth open and thrust his tongue deeply into her. His cock brushed her bare thigh and her fingers greedily curled around its length. Nigel groaned as she stroked him and tightened her fingers around his erection.

Lynette bent at her knees and took the ruby head between her lips. Her pussy was so wet and she needed to drive him as insane as she felt. Nigel's words bred courage in her to just do whatever she pleased. Right then, she wanted to suck his cock and make him groan.

"Yes, Lynette!" His hands were on her head, urging her to take more of his cock into her mouth. She stroked the length that she couldn't take, twisting her hand as she used her tongue on the large head. His breathing rasped between his teeth as his hips thrust forward with little jerky motions. "I'm going to come in your mouth."

"Yes!" She opened her mouth wider and sucked his cock deeper as his hips drove it between her lips and fingers. She wanted him to climax under her touch while she listened to the evidence of her own power over him. A harsh grunt hit her ears as his hand tightened in her hair and his seed hit her mouth. She purred as she licked and sucked all of his ejaculation from his cock.

"Sweet Lynette." His words floated over her head as he released her hair. He scooped her off her feet and laid her on the bed as he lay beside her, propped on one elbow. His eyes moved over her body as he cupped each breast and pinched the nipples gently. Her hips twitched as her pussy burned hotter.

"Turn over." The bed moved as he rose from it and opened one of the drawers to the dresser. He took a small jar from it and something that looked like a baby's pacifier, only thicker and longer. He held the thing up for her to see.

"I'm going to use this to stretch your bottom. You can't take a lover until you've used a plug first."

Her eyes rounded in shock but Nigel stroked her cheek. "Turn over, Lynette, I will not hurt you." She trusted him and knew it at that moment. She had liked everything else that he did to her so there was no reason to deny him this.

Rolling over, she turned her head to watch him.

"Draw your knees up under your body." She did it and felt her face flame as her bottom rose into the air. "Good girl, now spread your thighs for me."

It was such a vulnerable position. She was at his mercy and a little tingle of fear shot through her. But it mixed with the excitement, making her even more desperate to comply because she needed him to fuck her so very badly.

He opened the jar and dipped his finger into it. His skin glistened as he removed it and she felt the smooth glide of some fluid on her bottom. Nigel dipped into the jar again as he spread the cheeks of her bottom apart and then smoothed more of the lubricant over her back entrance.

"Your pussy smells so hot." She moaned softly as her body burned and Nigel dipped his finger into the jar again. She was burning with need and he was moving so slowly!

She jerked slightly as he inserted his finger into her bottom this time. A little shush came from his lips as he clamped his opposite hand around her hip to hold her steady. "Once I place this plug in your bottom, your pussy will be so tight, Lynette. My cock will make you scream as I fuck you."

She panted at the image, pushing her bottom towards his finger as he worked it in and out of her bottom. As she relaxed, it didn't feel so large anymore but easily slipped inside her. Nigel pulled his finger free and picked up the plug. He dipped it into the jar and then lifted its glittering length up and fitted it against her bottom.

The walls of her pussy were pressed against each other as he pushed the plug into her bottom. She whimpered as it stretched and pushed further into her. But she was crying with the need for more. She needed his cock inside her too.

"Fuck me, Nigel." The plug made her pussy burn so badly, she didn't care what he thought of her shameless demand. Only that he did what she wanted.

His hand smoothed over her bottom before he turned her over and thrust his cock into her. She screamed as climax ripped through her body. But it wasn't enough, her pussy still burned and his cock pressed deeply into her, filling her so tightly with the plug in her bottom.

Little wet sounds came from her body and she pushed her body up towards the hard thrust of his cock. The plug made her tight and pleasure shot up her spine with each thrust.

Nigel's eyes glowed with possession and her heart gave an odd twist. Being the object of his desire filled her with excitement, not anger as she thought it would have. There was a stark difference in the manner that Nigel meant to use her and appreciate her.

His eyes burned into hers as he thrust deeply into her pussy. "Do you like it?" He really wanted to know too. She could not have lied about anything at that moment because the pleasure was so intense, there was nothing but the sheer explosion of feelings that their flesh created. Her pussy demanded more and her hips lifted to offer his cock a smooth entry into her.

Nigel chuckled and pulled his cock free before thrusting back into her. "You see, Lynette? You will have to marry me because I'm not sure either of us could survive without this." He thrust hard into her spread body and then pulled free. He rolled over onto his back as she whimpered. She wasn't ready to stop! Her clit pulsed with the need to rub against his cock more.

"Ride me, Lynette."

Lynette rolled onto her side to look at Nigel. He was flat on his back and his cock thrust up from his body. A naughty grin was on his face as he offered her his hand. "Ride astride me, Lynette."

She giggled with excitement as she rolled onto her knees. Power was surging through her bloodstream, making her bold and brazen. She enjoyed every second of it too! The door was firmly shut and Nigel wasn't going to smear her name by telling the rest of the world about their escapades. She trusted him to keep their secret, but there was also the very real consequence of soiling his own name if he breathed a word to anyone.

She rose up and swung her thigh over his hips. It was a bit awkward but the head of his cock nudged her slit and she moaned as her body demanded she return to fucking him. Nigel's hand smoothed over the curve of her hip as his other hand grasped his cock and held it aimed at her pussy opening.

"Now lower your body." She did, and his cock thrust up into her, but she was the one controlling the speed. Nigel let his cock go and slid his hand up to one of her breasts. "Lean forward, Lynette. I want to see your little nipples bounce as you ride me."

"Yes, Nigel." She purred the words again and his eyes shot to her face as one dark eyebrow rose. "Hmm...and if you don't fuck me fast enough, I'll have to give you a touch of the whip, won't I? Just like a mare." His eyes darkened with desire as he bucked under her. "Clasp me with your thighs!"

His order rang out in the dark morning air as his hand rose and landed with a smack on her bottom. The blow surprised her and she jumped, pulling her body off his cock. The hand on her hip tightened to keep her from rising too far. The sting from his smack actually zipped into her pussy, making it clench with more need.

Lynette plunged back down onto his length and he chuckled. But it wasn't a nice sound, it was dark and very male and unless she missed her guess…authoritarian.

"Faster! I'm not some vapor-prone lady!" Another smack landed on her other cheek as she rose above him and then sent her body back onto his cock. Pleasure slammed into her belly as she was stretched on his cock. The plug in her bottom made it so tight she gasped.

Another smack on her bare bottom made the walls of her pussy clench around his length and she laughed as the pleasure swirled through her, banishing everything but the desire to obey.

Lynette set a good pace as she rose and fell. Her breasts bounced with the action as Nigel landed another smack on her bottom. He would change sides each time he smacked her flesh and the side not receiving attention actually longed for it as the opposite cheek received its share.

Nigel's nostrils flared as he released her hip and cupped one of her jiggling breasts. "Fuck me, Lynette." He snarled the order as his breath rasped between his clenched teeth. Climax was demanding she surrender to it but the power to be the one in control battled for her to hold off and ride Nigel until he came.

But control wasn't going to remain in her grasp. She slammed down onto that cock as his hand smacked her bottom again. Nigel grunted as he grabbed her hip and bucked beneath her. She felt the hot spurt of his seed erupting deep inside her body and climax ripped through her body as Nigel bucked under her spread thighs.

Sweet mercy, she needed a bath! Lynette opened her eyes and giggled as she thought that. Perspiration had coated her skin as she rode Nigel... Ladies did not sweat!

Yet she did and the man lying beside her offered her a grin as he twisted a lock of her hair around one finger. "I did warn you."

"Indeed you did." He had not been a gentleman, thank God.

Nigel rolled up onto one of his elbows and stared down into her face. He dropped her hair and lightly traced her lower lip with the tip of his finger. His eyes were intense as they lingered on her face and then down to her bare breasts. She didn't try to cover them, it was her body and at that moment she found herself well content with it.

He trailed that finger down her neck and over the swell of her breast until he circled the nipple. The little rose tip drew slowly into a tightened button despite the waves of satisfaction washing through her body.

"Do you have any idea how delightfully surprised I am to meet this side of you, Lynette?" Nigel lifted his eyes from her nipple and stared into hers. "I may lock you away in this lodge until your belly is round with my child, if you refuse to marry me."

Lynette believed him too. There was no mistaking the look in his eyes. It sent a bolt of emotion straight through her heart. It would be so simple for him to walk away now that she had yielded her body completely to his whim.

"All right, I will think about it."

His hand cupped her breast and gently squeezed it. "Then I must make sure to give you plenty of good examples to plead my case."

"Indeed you should." Their proper words made her giggle as Nigel dipped his head to lick her nipple.

One corner of his mouth lifted just a tiny amount as his eyes darkened. He tapped her lips with his fingertip. "I will ask you again tomorrow."

"Why tomorrow?"

His hand smoothed over her cheek. "Because I have needs, Lynette, that you haven't witnessed yet. I won't hold you to your promise if you cannot accept me completely."

A current of excitement flowed through her again. The needs that he had already introduced her to were beyond anything that she might have imagined, but his words sparked an increasing hunger for more...more...of what she didn't know, only that she craved it.

"I'm hungry, Nigel, I believe you should feed me."

He groaned low and deep, making her nipples draw tighter. Desire brightened his eyes as his mouth lowered to hers and demanded entry. He lifted his head and grinned at her like a boy once again. "As my lady wishes."

Oh, she did wish for it! She wanted him to lock her away behind the closed door and feed her until she was plump on satisfaction and pleasure. A shiver raced up her spine as Nigel left the bed to retrieve the basket on the table. His words were bouncing around inside her head as she tried to consider what more there was to explore. The plug was still in her bottom, making her pussy tight.

Would Nigel really share her? Dare she let anyone else know how much she enjoyed the sins of the flesh? The idea simmered in her imagination as she battled the urge to sink further into Nigel's needs.

It was possible she might never emerge.

Chapter Five

ॐ

Her enjoyment only paled as she sat down to another cup of Celeste's bitter tea. The world was unforgiving and Nigel had returned them to the house in time for a late afternoon tea.

"You must drink it, Lynette." Anna sat an empty cup onto its delicate saucer as she aimed disapproving eyes at Lynette. She raked her gaze down to Lynette's waist and fluttered her eyelashes in warning. "You wouldn't want to lose that tiny waist."

Lynette suddenly looked at the concoction in her cup and tried to keep her jaw from dropping. She had heard rumors of ladies taking...*measures* to prevent babies, but she had never actually met a lady who did it.

Until now. Celeste's words of the day before floated through her memory as she lifted the cup and swallowed another portion. Celeste was starting a family after this weekend and would have no more of the tea.

"You are very dear to think of me." Lynette finished off her cup as she smiled gracefully at her two friends. That knowing look was back in Celeste's eyes as she smiled back.

"We are closer than sisters now, Lynette."

Excitement twisted her stomach as Anna and Celeste both rose. They both knew more about tonight than she did. Lynette could feel their tension as they walked past the maids and into the hallway. Celeste turned to Lynette as Anna began to climb the stairs.

"I'm sure you will want to bathe after your ride this morning. I told the upstairs maid to see to it before supper. But George wants to dine privately tonight so I will bid you good night now. Pleasant dreams."

Celeste dropped a kiss onto her cheek and left. Apprehension joined the excitement brewing in her blood as Lynette climbed the stairs towards her room. Nigel would find her tonight, she was certain of it.

A bathing tub was waiting in her chamber. Lynette smiled as she let the waiting maid disrobe her. After the heat of the day, a bath would be divine. She had to control a naughty smile that threatened to break through her calm composure. After her morning ride, a bath was very much needed! The evening was even warm enough that she might wash her hair and let it dry without fearing a head chill.

Half an hour later, Lynette stood just inside the veranda's open doors. The night breeze blew in as she pulled a silver brush through her wet hair. A loose dressing gown was tied around her body. She wore nothing else.

Lynette smiled—her breasts felt so decadent. The skin tingled as a memory of Nigel's hands on them rose from her memory. Being completely naked had been so very decadent. Even her bare toes felt delightful as she indulged herself in a moment of pure sensation. The breeze found its way down her robe, making her smile even more.

She was only slightly sore but it did not compare to the steady pulse of need that was now her constant companion. Maybe it had always been there, flowing through her veins, ignorance masking what it really was. Now she understood and there was a relief that came with that knowledge. It was almost like she hadn't known herself and had lived her life with her eyes tightly shut to avoid looking at her own face.

Lynette sighed as a small rap landed on the chamber door. The maid would be returning to dress her. Turning about, she allowed the household staff to put her to bed. The thick curtains were drawn before the maid left for the night.

The maid's steps had just disappeared when a curtain moved and Celeste's face peeked into the bed. She carried a single candle in one hand and held it carefully away from the bed hangings.

"Stuff two pillows under the bedding and come with me." A rather naughty smile curved across her face as Lynette fought with her nightgown to get her legs out from beneath the thick coverlet.

Lynette crawled out of the bed and stepped down beside Celeste. Her friend reached up and made sure the bed curtains were tightly closed again.

"There. I must have a bolt installed on this chamber's door but this will serve for tonight. Even if one of those silly maids gets the idea to look in on you, those pillows look just like you in the dark."

"Am I not sleeping here?"

Celeste smiled brightly as her eyes flashed in the meager light. She reached for Lynette's hand and clasped it as she began walking towards the far end of the chamber.

"Dear Lynette, I invited you to a party and it's just beginning. Let's not be late, Nigel will come looking for you himself and have no care for your good name."

That he would! Lynette didn't doubt it but then being locked in that hunting lodge wouldn't be such a cruel fate either.

Reaching the wall, Celeste pushed on one of the fireplace's ornately carved sides. It pushed in to reveal a doorway of sorts.

"You must push on the angel's face. Tomorrow night, as soon as the maid has left, come and join us. Tell the maid to leave you a candle to read by. It's dark in the passage."

The single candle illuminated a hallway as Celeste made certain the opening next to the fireplace was sealed. Her friend led her down a passage. Another door was sealed in front of them. But it was plain and simple to see the place in the center that would open it.

The door moved to show a room lit with more candles. It wasn't brightly lit as a room would be for visitors. Instead, there was a golden glow with just enough light to make the room a tapestry of shadows and flickering light.

"There you are, my dear."

Celeste's husband was leaning against a pillar in the round-shaped room with a crystal decanter of brandy in his hand. Lynette felt her eyes go round as she looked at George. He had only a pair of under trousers on. Nothing else. To see such an upstanding gentleman of society thus was frankly...unheard of.

He smiled a warm smile at Lynette before he let his eyes drop down her length. He sat the glass aside before striding over to capture his wife in a strong embrace. They kissed in open mouth fashion. Celeste hummed in her throat when her husband lifted his lips from hers.

George released his wife to capture the side of Lynette's face in his hand.

"I was completely delighted to hear you would be joining our little soirées." His arm captured her exactly as he had done with his wife. Their bodies collided as he lowered his mouth and firmly kissed her. Lynette gasped and he thrust his tongue deeply into her open mouth. Heat rushed down her body as the very firm bulge of his cock pressed against her tummy. Guilt tugged at her as she tried to turn away from the kiss and search the room for Nigel.

"Give over, George. I've wanted a taste of her since she hit the season three years ago."

George's head lifted as Lynette found herself turned into another man's embrace. She caught just a brief glimpse of Henry Gilmore's face before the man kissed her as well. His tongue thrust into her mouth as Lynette felt her blood heat even further. Another hard cock was pressing into her belly, making her passage warm and moist.

She sent her tongue to stroke along the one probing her mouth. Henry groaned and let a hand slip over a cheek of her bottom.

Henry lifted his lips to smile approvingly at her. "I see you definitely belong with us, my dear."

Lifting her eyes, Lynette considered the room. Another man leaned against a wall as his dark eyes were watching her. Recognition was instant. She almost felt him as much as she saw him.

Nigel's eyes darkened as he took a few steps towards her. In stark contrast to the other men in the room, he was clothed. He tapped his boot with a riding crop as his eyes traveled over her body with precise motions. Lynette was only wearing her nightgown and she didn't care. Celeste and Anna were wearing less. But there was a guarded nature about Nigel just then. He was watching her to see what she made of the event.

"Will you take that sack off, Lynette?"

Celeste laughed deeply before appearing at Lynette's side. "He's a daring one. Nigel always likes to look at his toys before he plays with them." Her friend smiled before pulling a ribbon tie on the neck of Lynette's nightgown. "Go on, take it off. I simply can't wait any longer to have you become one of us."

Celeste's hand lifted Lynette's chin 'til their eyes met. "You do understand, my dear, we all have needs and that's what true friends are for? It's much safer this way. The servants talk and we simply can't have that. We'll keep your secret and you'll keep ours."

A smile brightened Lynette's face. A twin one appeared on Celeste's face. There was no need to fear being tossed out of society. Not if she embraced those who held the same urges. Lynette felt the slide of fluid on her bare thighs as she considered the three men in the room. Their state of undress told her they held no reservations about feeding either her hunger or their own.

But she stared back at Nigel as she lifted the hem of her gown and tossed it aside. She was beautiful to him, and that morning she had seen the proof on his face. If sharing her was his need then she would embrace it as well, as long as he was near.

"Once again you leave me no reason to punish you, Lynette." The tip of the riding crop appeared under her chin. Nigel's eyes were bright with hunger as he reached for one of her nipples. "That displeases me greatly."

A shiver raced down her back as Anna giggled and turned to Celeste's husband. The two began kissing as Celeste was hauled into Henry's embrace. Nigel's eyes captured hers again. The riding crop lowered to slap against his boot again.

"Touch your breasts, Lynette, show me how you like to be touched. Let your hands be your lover."

He backed up a step to watch her. Lynette hesitated as she lifted her fingers to the top swell of her breasts. Being so completely on display made her hands shake. Excitement bubbled up her body, yet it was tempered with nervousness.

A throb hit her passage as she looked at the dark eyes of Nigel Spencer. Need rose up as she let her gaze wander down his body. She stroked her fingertips down each breast until she found her own nipples. Her hands moved over the little buttons as she cupped each breast from underneath. Nigel's eyes followed with devotion once again. She obeyed yet he was the slave.

The cool night air brushed her skin, making her smile. What a delicious sensation. Her skin was alive with tiny pulses of feeling and for once, she wasn't covered and laced into endless layers of fabric.

Nigel's eyes traveled over her body as he slowly circled her. Lynette felt her skin flush as he made a complete survey of her nude body. Nigel wore a pair of black leather riding boots. The heels tapped with each slow step he took.

"Anna my dear, I've missed your clever tongue."

Lynette tilted her head to see Anna on her knees in front of Celeste's husband, George. She was as naked as Lynette was, and on her knees with the man's engorged penis between her lips. She sucked on the head of the cock as her slim hands gripped the rod.

Celeste didn't seem to mind the other woman's attentions on her husband. Henry was sucking on her large coral nipples as he gripped the cheeks of her bottom.

A sharp blow landed on her own bottom from the riding crop. Lynette jumped and glared at Nigel. He held the rod over his chest as he frowned deeply at her.

"You will watch me, Lynette." The crop snapped on his boot again. "Or be punished."

"Will I?" Her bottom stung from the blow, but the sounds of Anna's sucking were tempting her to watch the other couple. Just the wet sounds of her sucking a cock made her pussy pulse with the need to be fucked.

"Yes."

"Damn fine luck you've got, Nigel. Poor girl is quite clearly in love with you," Henry muttered before sweeping Celeste off her feet and walking past Lynette's eyes to a chaise lounge that sat in the corner. He laid Celeste on the brocade-covered lounge and dropped to his knees between her legs. The candlelight shimmered across them as he leaned forward to suck on her slit.

"I rather like the idea of having a wife that is in love with me." Nigel's eyes glowed with possession as he swept a finger over one of her breasts. He leaned forward and sucked the nipple between his lips. Heat flowed from her nipple to her pussy as the tip of his tongue worried the puckered nub.

The riding crop hit the boot again with a sharp sound. Nigel lifted his mouth from her breast and grinned at her. "You will follow my orders tonight, Lynette."

"And what if I do not choose to obey you? You are not my husband."

A harsh look crossed Nigel's face before he cupped her chin in his warm hand. He leaned forward until his breath teased her lips with the promise of a kiss. Her pussy clenched as her body erupted into an inferno of heat. Everything flowed into her belly, making her long for the deep penetration only a cock could provide.

"If you disobey me, I won't fuck you."

Lynette gasped. She needed him already. Her thighs were slick with her own juices and he'd barely touched her. He laughed deep in his chest before running his hand down her neck and over her bare breast. He stopped at the nipple and captured it between a thumb and finger. "And you will marry me, Lynette. Celeste is already planning the reception."

"Um...it will be delightful, Lynette. July sometime." Celeste gasped and moaned as Henry thrust one of his thick fingers into her pussy. Her head fell back onto the bed as he worked that digit in and out of her body. Nigel moved closer and nipped her ear with his teeth before whispering to her.

"Do you feel it, Lynette? The surge of life? Henry, George and I were always together as boys. I think we lost our virginity with the same slut. This is why I've never joined the gentlemen courting during the season. I needed you to be here, to understand that the pleasure of the body is not twisted."

Nigel stood behind her and rolled one of her nipples between his finger and thumb, pleasure shot into her belly. He pinched it, making her gasp with surprise. It wasn't truly pain. The sensation was so very intense. Lynette couldn't keep her body from reacting. "I want to watch Henry lap your slit."

She moaned as she watched Henry insert two fingers into Celeste's spread body. Her own pussy quivered with the need to lie down on that bed. He would be her lover and Nigel would watch them. The idea made her shiver as it taunted her with the pleasure to be gained.

"I see I have captured your attention, dear Lynette. Think about it. I could suck you and rub you but never fuck you. We have rules, you see. No one gets to ride that little pussy until my cock does. The three of us could suck you all night long but save our fucking for Anna and Celeste."

Nigel released her nipple and pulled his shirt over his head. His chest was sculpted to perfection. A light coat of dark hair ran across his chest and down to his belly.

Celeste let out a deep moan as Henry's lapping sounds became much louder. Nigel's eyes were trained on her face. Lynette smiled at his game. The party was a feast of the flesh, but it would appear there were many levels to satisfaction.

Nigel's dark eyes promised her something quite different tonight. He was going to teach her intimacy, both between them and between friends too.

"Yes, Nigel." She purred it exactly as she had that morning and his lips twitched into that boyish grin.

"Very good. Now, come and remove my boots."

She giggled a little as she bent over to pull the first boot off. Unlike their morning at the hunting lodge, she was bare now and her breasts hung free for Nigel's eyes as she pulled on the boot. Even more wicked was the idea that her legs were on either side of his which meant her bottom and pussy was displayed clearly to the men behind her.

"Ah, now my breeches."

Lynette felt her smile grow. Moving forward, she reached for the fastening at the waistband.

"Pull them down my legs and stay on your knees."

The trousers came free quite easily. Lynette found it simple to pull them to the floor when she did as he told her and dropped to her knees.

"Now fold them and put them under your knees."

Lynette didn't move. Nigel's cock was jutting out at her face and her mouth watered for a taste of it. She ran her hand over its rigid length as she parted her lips to taste its ruby head. The riding crop cut through the air and smacked her bottom.

A small cry escaped her lips as she glared up at Nigel. He raised an eyebrow and firmly stroked the length of his staff as she watched. Lynette felt her lips go dry as she considered the monster impaling her.

"Tsk, tsk, Lynette, now I have a reason to punish you. Should I confess I was looking for one? I enjoyed smacking your ass this morning."

She had too. Their eyes meet as she recalled the way her body had responded to his "punishment". It had made her pussy even hotter. Right then the sting from his blows was zipping into her pussy and making more fluid seep down its walls. The need to fuck was growing beyond her ability to control.

She reached for the trousers and placed them under her knees. It made the position much more comfortable. His cock was inches from her face, giving her the chance to look at the swollen head in detail. The ruby head was as large as a plum and the staff had to be eight inches long, at least.

"Spread your knees apart, my dear, and open that little mouth."

He pushed the head of his cock into her mouth. Lynette licked it with the same motions she'd used that morning. A small hum came from his chest as she lifted her hands to stroke the staff. She wanted to hear him groan with pleasure again and she wanted everyone else in the room to hear it too.

"Take it deeper." Nigel's hand held her head as he pushed his cock into her mouth.

"Relax and suck it harder."

Lynette groaned around the huge cock. He stretched her mouth with it and her pussy screamed for the same treatment.

The riding crop cut through the air, making her eyes pop wide open. Lynette knew the blow would land on her bottom. A sharp sting made her jump but Nigel held her head in place as he gently fucked her mouth.

"Where's that tongue?"

Another hiss from the riding crop and her opposite cheek stung. Lynette sent her tongue over the head of the staff. His hips gently moved as she licked and sucked at the same time. Her bottom smarted but the sensation suddenly turned into acute hunger as the smacks intensified the throbbing in her pussy.

"That's it. I want both on my cock. Lick the head and open wider for me."

Lynette was almost desperate to please him. Her body was a single flame and she needed him to feed the blaze of need. The ragged edge of his voice fed her own ego as she licked and swallowed more of his engorged cock.

The riding crop hissed and struck. Nigel's hips thrust and he smacked her other cheek. His breath was hard as he increased his pace and sent the riding crop towards her bottom again.

"Give her your load, Nigel!"

Lynette didn't know who spoke and she didn't care. She sucked harder as the cock was buried in her mouth so deeply, she couldn't breathe. Her bottom was on fire as another smack landed. Nigel pulled out and she sucked in a breath as her tongue frantically licked his staff.

Thick seed hit her tongue as Nigel groaned and shuddered. The hot spurt of his seed made her greedy. Lynette sucked even harder on his cock. She couldn't let him go slack. She wanted to be fucked!

"Would you look at her go?"

"Damn, I can't wait for my turn!"

Nigel pulled out of her mouth abruptly. Henry and George stood with their cocks jutting out from their bodies. She sat there on her knees as her pride rushed forward. There might be sharing in her next marriage but Nigel would be her first lover!

Celeste suddenly appeared and rubbed her hand over Henry's stiff staff. She lifted the rod towards Lynette as Henry stepped forward. "Go on, dear, we all share."

Lynette opened her mouth and found a second cock nestled inside it. She reached for the rod with her hands as she licked the head and sucked it further inside. Her eyes popped open again as she caught sight of Nigel beneath her.

His head appeared between her spread knees. He ran a thick finger through the folds of her sex, making her groan.

"Keep sucking Henry. If you stop, I'll stop."

His hot tongue lapped her slit next. Lynette groaned as her passage clenched tightly. Henry caught her head and pushed his cock into her mouth. Nigel pulled the folds of her sex open before licking around the opening to her pussy.

It was all so much. Almost too much. Lynette forced herself to keep sucking as Nigel found the nub at the top of her sex and sucked it into his mouth. His large hand moved over her bottom in a soothing motion as climax seemed to twist her body. Suddenly Henry's cock delivered a load of seed into her mouth as Nigel sucked harder on her sex. Pleasure split her in two as she writhed between both men.

"Goddamn, but she's got a wicked tongue."

Another cock nudged her lips and Lynette gladly opened her mouth for George. Nigel was still lapping her slit and fire blazed up her body as she surrendered to the pure indulgence of the party.

Under the attention, she blossomed. Gaining confidence to seek out what she wanted. Her fingers tightened around a hard cock as she used her mouth to make George groan. Yes, she burned for possession but she also craved this power to return that pleasure to another.

To a man.

Lying beneath her husband had been so lonely. How did you spread your thighs, allowing a man to fuck you and never stroke his skin? Never hear his breath rasp between his lips as his body battled against his control.

She craved that as much as the deep thrust inside her own body. Moving her hand down the length of George's cock, she cupped the twin sacs at its base and his hips jerked. She sent her tongue around the head of his cock as he gasped and shot his seed into her mouth.

Lynette rose from her knees as George offered her a shaky smile. Pride shot through her as she watched the man waver on his feet. Her eyes locked with Nigel's as she noticed that he had watched her the entire time. His eyes burned with an emotion that lit a similar fire inside her heart. It was a companionship that was far deeper than any friendship she had ever known. Here they were honest with each other. Not hiding behind society's rules and ideas of perfection.

Instead they made their own rapture. Embracing that primitive beast that was always locked away. It was a stolen moment of bliss and Lynette decided she was going to become a thief.

Chapter Six

ഔ

"George, you didn't last even half as long in her mouth."

Anna laughed as George collapsed onto one of the lounges. Lynette shivered as Nigel released her body and rose to his feet. He extended a hand to her and she gratefully left her knees. But a smile curved her lips as she witnessed all three men smiling at her. She could suck a cock as well as any maid in her house!

Nigel led her to a bed at the far end of the room. Lynette eagerly followed him onto it. Despite climaxing twice, her body still yearned for true completion. Nigel's dark eyes didn't promise her that ultimate pleasure just yet.

Henry followed them and pushed Lynette back until he was able to spread her legs apart.

"What a sweet little pussy you have." His eyes inspected her body a moment. Henry grinned at her before he lowered his head and lapped her slit. Pleasure shot up her body as the man lapped and licked and sucked on her open sex. The wet sounds hit her ears as Nigel began sucking on her nipples. Anna appeared and began suckling Nigel's cock.

Her body twisted again as climax loomed over her. Lynette gasped as Nigel's dark eyes bore into hers and his ragged breathing told her he was in the same torment.

He leaned forward and captured her mouth in a kiss as her body erupted into climax. He groaned as he deepened the kiss. Both of their chests rose and fell as they tried to catch their breaths.

Henry rose above her with his member swollen and hard. He hesitated over her spread body but climbed over the bed and came up behind Anna. She had simply leaned over the bed to suck Nigel's erection. Henry growled softly before bending his wife over the bed. His hips thrust forward as Lynette heard the wet sounds of deep penetration.

Anna's face became a mask of pleasure. She clawed at the bedding as Henry fucked her from behind. She cried and begged but Henry seemed unwilling to let climax overtake him.

Nigel's dark eyes were heavy with hunger. Lynette couldn't stand it anymore.

"Fuck me."

He laughed and pinched her nipple. Lynette swatted his hand away.

"Should I ask George?"

Nigel's eyes turned hard. He rolled over his shoulder and between her legs. Anna cried again as Henry began fucking her harder.

Nigel let the head of his cock rest against the opening to her passage. Lynette strained forward as she tried to take it into her body.

"Do you hate me?"

He meant his needs. Lynette propped herself up on her elbows as she let the sound of the couple fucking right next to her fire her blood. "I believe I am falling in love with you."

Nigel thrust hard into her and her body jerked. Her pussy stretched around his cock as pleasure spiked through her body. Nigel pulled out and thrust forward as Lynette tipped her hips up for his possession. "I fuck you first and last, Lynette, always. But I want to watch your face as you ride George. He'll want your bottom, not your pussy." A whimper came from her throat as she remembered the plug and how tight it had made her pussy.

"Should we fuck you at the same time? George in your bottom and my cock in your pussy?"

"Yes!" It was the only word she could think of. Yes, she wanted to be fucked. Yes, she needed him to keep pumping that monster into her pussy. Yes, Yes, Yes!

Climax was hard. It ripped into her as she tried to shove his cock even deeper into her body. Anna begged again but Henry simply laughed.

"I'm going to fuck you until you can't walk, my dear!" Henry slapped her bottom before turning her and lifting her to the bed. Anna spread her thighs for her husband as he immediately began working his cock in and out of her body.

Nigel suddenly stopped and pulled out of her body. He reached for her hip and rolled her onto her tummy. Lynette's legs closed as she rolled and Nigel immediately pushed them open. His fingers dipped deeply into her passage before withdrawing and running up between the cheeks of her bottom.

"Pull your knees beneath you, my dear, but keep the knees apart."

Lynette assumed the position as he spoke. Her eyes were riveted to George and Celeste across the room. George was sitting in a chair with his feet on the floor. Celeste was on the man's lap with her knees on either side of his hips. She rose up and down as George spanked her. Celeste would moan as she slid down the length of George's erection but sob as his hand smacked her bottom. She rose with the blow and then plunged back down the length of the rod as she returned to moaning.

"I'm going to use a larger plug in your bottom, Lynette. After you take it, you'll be ready for a cock." Nigel stroked her bottom with a sure hand before dipping his finger into her pussy again. He returned to her bottom and carried her thick juices to the tiny back entrance of her body.

Celeste began to moan in earnest. There was a frantic bounce to her riding as she ground her hips down onto George's lap. She gasped and cried out as George watched through bright eyes. Lust still raged across George's face. He stood up and placed Celeste on her feet. His cock was still swollen as he bent Celeste over the side table. Celeste immediately spread her feet. She raised her bottom as George dipped his fingers into a small jar next to her hand.

"You see? George prefers the bottom for his cock."

Lynette shivered as Nigel's words floated past her ear. Could she really do that? Taking Nigel's stiff cock into her pussy was the natural order of things but in her bottom? George smeared fluid over Celeste's bottom before thrusting two of his fingers into her. He wiggled the digits and worked them deeply into the woman bent over in front of him.

Celeste turned her head to smile at Lynette as George removed his hand and applied more lubricant to her bottom. She bit her lip as George began to penetrate her. His hands were firmly wrapped over each of her slim hips as he drove his stiff cock into her bottom.

Nigel slowly invaded her own bottom with a finger at the same time. Lynette jumped but his hand was also wrapped around one of her hips and he controlled her body, keeping it in position.

"Relax, my dear. Push your bottom up higher." Nigel reached past her to a small table next to the bed. Lynette stared at the items lying there. She quickly scanned the rest of the chamber. There was a similar set of items on each and every table. Celeste had clearly held such parties before.

There was a small jar of some form of lubricant. It was already open and Nigel's fingers dipped into it. The candlelight glistened off his wet fingers as he lifted his hand. Next to the jar was a small plug exactly like the one Nigel had pressed into her bottom that morning. It was four inches long and quite thick. It wasn't the only one. There was another lying there that was another inch longer and much thicker. Both had loops on the ends and Lynette felt a shiver run down her back as she considered that the loop would be the only part of the plug outside her bottom.

The hand on her hip made a soothing motion in response. Lynette felt Nigel return to her bottom with the lubricant. His fingers brushed and circled her opening before thrusting inside again. She ached as the skin stretched. He wiggled the digits and pushed further into her. Her pussy suddenly began to pulse as its walls were pushed together by Nigel's fingers.

"Very good, Lynette. You really are quite a hot little piece. You will drink Celeste's tea every day for at least a year. I need to fuck you that long before we have a baby and I have to treat you gently."

Lynette gasped. She wasn't sure a year was long enough or that she would be able to endure gentle treatment from Nigel knowing the heights of pleasure his rough handling could take her to.

"Don't worry, Lynette, I will still fuck you despite pregnancy. We shall just have to limit our excesses."

His fingers dipped into the jar again and returned to her bottom. He worked them in and out of her quite easily now. The sensation made her pussy heat again.

"Do you understand now, Lynette? I enjoy sharing. You are the rarest of treasures. Polished and poised on the exterior, but delightfully in touch with your feminine core."

Nigel reached for the table but picked up the larger plug this time. He dipped it into the jar before carrying it to her bottom. Lynette shuddered as she felt the first inch of the thing enter her bottom. Nigel smoothed her hip but thrust forward as she writhed.

Suddenly her bottom stretched. The plug was pushed into position as she began burning for a deep fucking once more. A moan of pure sensation rose out of her throat. She could never have imagined how hot the plug would make her.

"She took it?"

"Splendidly." Nigel turned her over as Henry gently smoothed his hand over her bottom to look at the small loop. He smiled with lust as his hand absently stroked his swollen member. His cock wasn't as thick or long as Nigel's, yet it still appeared to be of good size.

Henry leaned down and sucked part of her pussy into his mouth. His tongue rubbed the bud of her sex as he continued to suck on her. Two thick fingers thrust into her pussy, making her moan. She was burning alive! With the plug in her bottom, the finger filled her, making her desperate for more friction.

"What a hot little box you have. Nigel, I think it's my turn. I've warmed Anna up for you. Go stretch her with that cock of yours."

Nigel laughed and rolled onto his back. His cock thrust up into the air. Anna appeared and fashioned her mouth around the head of his member. Nigel's hand twisted into her hair as he urged her to take more of his weapon.

Henry thrust his fingers into Lynette's pussy again. His eyes watched as he fucked her with the digits. He smiled at her before removing his fingers and fitting his penis into her body. He slowly thrust into her. Lynette whimpered as her body seemed too tight for his cock. But he pushed forward as his hands held her hips in place.

"Ah yes! What a hot pussy you have!"

Henry buried his cock in her to the hilt. He rode her hard. His hips hammered into her as she lifted her bottom to deepen the penetration. Pleasure shot out from each thrust as the plug in her bottom intensified every stroke of his cock.

Pleasure spiked through her too many times to count. Lynette listened to the slap of Henry's body against her own as she watched Anna mount Nigel. It was decadent and overindulgent, yet in the end, it satisfied her craving. The inner need she had to be filled was sated.

* * * * *

She drifted into slumber sometime in the early morning hours. Her head against Nigel's chest and it was the oddest comfort she had ever felt. His fingers played with a lock of her hair as their legs twisted and her thigh ended up draped over his.

Nigel groaned and moved, making her frown, two little tears pricking her eyelids as he left her. It was a strange emotional response but she wanted his body next to hers.

"Come, Lynette, I cannot let the maids find you missing." He hated that truth. Nigel scooped her off the bed and stood her on her feet. He scanned the room looking for her nightgown as he battled the urge to saddle a team and whisk her off to a chapel for a dawn wedding.

He couldn't do that to her. Even if her belly didn't swell with child, the old crows would whisper behind their fans that she had miscarried or lied to him to catch his fortune.

Three months would be long enough, and practically eternity for him. Being near her soothed his inner beast. She fed his cravings like a wolf bringing in fresh meat for her litter.

Lynette frowned as her nightgown fell over her body. She hated the fabric and even more the idea that her body needed to be covered. Nigel smoothed a hand over her hair as he picked her up and left the chamber. She sighed as her head found his chest again and her ear detected the steady beat of his heart.

There was nothing but contentment right then. Nigel carried her to the chamber that was hers and shouldered the curtains aside before laying her among the bedding. His mouth found hers as he kissed her deeply. Passion didn't stir from the kiss but she felt it deeply as tender emotion filled her heart.

"I hate to leave you, Lynette." She lifted her drowsy eyes and saw that truth reflected in his stare. He looked lonely as he tucked the covers up to her chin and smoothed them over her chest.

"Three months, Lynette, and don't let your mother tell you any different." He stood up and aimed a hard stare at her as his order hung over her head. Lynette sighed as she rolled onto her side and smiled at him.

"Yes, Nigel…" She purred the words and blew him a kiss before he closed the bed curtains and Lynette surrendered to fatigue. Contentment surged through her as her brain drifted into deep sleep.

No guilt or worry that she had failed to please. There was only a steady glow burning through her heart that she was exactly what Nigel wanted her to be and he the most perfect man she could ever have met.

Maybe that was what love was.

* * * * *

Lynette crawled from her bed when the maid pulled the curtains aside. Daylight streamed into the room and with it came a flood of social responsibilities. Lynette didn't mind. Her feet were light as she stood for dressing.

"Madam is in a fine mood today. It was a good night?"

Lynette felt the slightest jump of her heart before she firmly clamped her willpower over the response. The maid was simply being polite.

"Yes, the night was most pleasant."

Lynette smiled as the maid finished. Her body was slightly sore as she descended the stairs. It wasn't true pain. Instead, she was delightfully calm. Her hunger wasn't raging and distracting her from the day's duties.

"Good morning, Lynette." Celeste smiled over her sweet bread.

Breakfast was served on the open porch of the summer home. The large openings were covered with screens. Taking her seat, Lynette smiled at her host. All three ladies were poised and gentle as the staff served them their meal.

"Lynette dear, I understand you ride each morning. Celeste does have a fine stable." Anna gently fanned herself as she considered Lynette.

"I find myself most content in your company this morning."

"How lovely." Anna continued to fan as Celeste smiled.

The common conversation held deeper meaning as the ladies withdrew from the table. Lynette was more than content to spend her day in gentle pursuits.

"Well, we have work to do, Lynette! Your wedding will not plan itself." Celeste snapped her fan shut as she stood up.

Lynette frowned at her. "Why do I feel as though you have trapped me like a pheasant, Celeste?"

Anna smothered a laugh as Celeste fluttered her eyelashes in innocence. "Perhaps because I have, Lynette. Poor Nigel has been so lonely, I confess I was quite excited when I noticed that you shared similar interests with him."

Celeste leaned forward and pulled Lynette to her feet by her gloved hands. "Confess you have never enjoyed a weekend more or I shall never forgive you!"

"Oh I have confessions all right, Celeste, but I fear they are best saved for my silent prayers!"

Anna took one of Lynette's hands and pulled her towards the door. "What better reason to marry, Lynette? You had no tender affection in your first marriage, was that any better?"

"I see your point." Nigel's words floated through her memory... *Love always gets its roots from lust...* Hmm, it was an interesting idea that grew in her mind until she believed it.

Anna laughed as they all left and the maids grinned as they cleared the table. They couldn't help thinking that ladies were certainly different from them. To marry a man that you had so briefly met, now where was the sense in that? They shook their heads as they took the dishes to the kitchen and offered the doormen a glimpse of their ankles on the way.

Well, ladies wouldn't understand that either, but a serving girl needed to take her pleasure when she could. Life was hard for a working girl and there wouldn't be any grand courtships for them, but that didn't mean there couldn't be a good spot of fun from time to time.

Gentlefolks wouldn't understand, their blood was too thin.

Chapter Seven

∽

"I bid you good night." Lynette rose with a fluid motion from her seat beside Celeste. The after-dinner lounge was painfully boring. The most interesting thing of the entire evening was the fact that Lynette now understood the tiny clues that told her Celeste and Anna shared her view of the strict social regimen.

But that wasn't her true problem.

Nigel. She sighed over his name. She had not laid an eye on the man all day. It shouldn't concern her. Paul had never spent much time with her but there was an odd ache centered in her heart that refused to mind her logic on the matter.

Celeste's lips were pinched into a pleasant smile while Anna continued to fan herself well beyond any heat. Lynette was at her limit of hiding her longings for Nigel.

"Good night, dear."

Both ladies rose with Lynette. Their faces immediately brightened with the prospect of the evening ending. Both smiled secretly at her as they cast lowered looks at their husbands across the room.

She risked everything by leaving her guest-bed to join the party in the inner chamber but she would do it again, she knew without doubt.

Still, Lynette felt her heart begin to accelerate as she considered what she might gain. Nigel would be there because his needs drove him to the group. She understood it now because she suffered the same thirst.

Boldness began to run through her bloodstream as she entered her sleeping chamber. A maid stepped forward to assist her with preparing for bed.

"I will sleep in my corset tonight. Tighten it."

It was not an uncommon request from a lady to her maid. With the current fashion, many girls slept in their stays to trim their figures into perfection. Lynette was set upon remaining in her stays for another reason though. She wanted to command Nigel tonight. If he wanted to see her body bared, then the man would maid her himself.

"Good night, madam." The maid closed the bed curtains and left.

Lynette waited for the door to close before she left the bed. A single candle burned on the nightstand, making her smile as she recalled Celeste instructing her to use it to join the true entertainment. She went to the door first to check that it was closed tight. No opening to let fingers of light spill into the hallway and give her away. No, that would not do. She would melt into the night like a shadow and meet the other dark shapes she found hiding there.

A floor-length looking glass stood next to the candle. Lynette considered her image. Her corset made her waist tiny. Her hips swelled out in rounded display as her breasts were thrust high. The shift she wore was whisper-thin and the light beams from the flame made it translucent.

Her hair streamed down her back, making her quite fetching. Except for the knickers she wore. Lynette made swift work of the bloomers and cast them aside. Now the beams from the candle illuminated her bare legs. Fluid was already easing from her pussy onto the top of her thighs. She was hot and ready to fling herself into the madness of the flesh again.

A shadow moved from the back of the room, making her spin around to face it. Nigel materialized from the darkness like a fantasy coming to life.

"I thought that maid would never leave."

He was completely bare. Her fingers glided across a chest that was warm and taut. He pressed her towards his body as his mouth descended and captured hers. The kiss was bold but controlled. Nigel thrust his tongue into her mouth to mingle with his.

Lynette stroked her tongue along the length of his as he captured the back of her head and held it prisoner to his kiss. His mouth was hot but so very slow. Nigel wasn't in any hurry to end the deep merging. He turned her head with his hand as he tasted every last bit of her mouth before lifting his head.

"I am beginning to see the merits of letting you keep certain bits of clothing, Lynette."

He smoothed his fingers over the mounds of her breasts. A shiver raced down her arms, raising gooseflesh as it went. Nigel's fingers reached into her stays to lift both of her breasts above the top of the garment. He leaned forward and licked one of her nipples and then the other. Lynette gasped as liquid fire ran down her body and into her pussy. Love and lust combined into a blaze that she'd never felt before.

Lynette found Nigel's flat nipples and gently pinched them. A deep shudder crossed his body as his hands cupped her breasts. Lynette reached down to catch the length of his cock in her hand. A mutter of delight escaped her lips as she held his member in her hand and felt it throb against her palm. Lynette worked her hand over the skin and smiled as Nigel's breathing became harsh.

"I missed you today."

He chuckled as he lifted the candle from the table and captured her hand in his. He turned and walked into the dark corner of the room, leaving the bed in darkness. He didn't move towards the carved angle, instead he opened a door that connected with the suite next to hers.

"Should I confess that I rode all the way back into Boston to see your father?" The candle was placed on a marble-topped table as Nigel turned to look at her. "Be angry if you like but you will wear my ring when you leave here."

Lynette wasn't sure what angered her more, his confession or the very real fact that she had to return home tomorrow. She couldn't stay mad though, happiness burned right through her pride's attempt to control her destiny. Maybe she had not quite believed the fact that Nigel really did intend to marry her. He certainly had every reason not to, according to her mother's teachings!

"Aren't we going to the party tonight?"

Nigel stroked the swells of her breasts again. "No. I want you a little more to myself tonight."

He stopped a mere breath from her body and took a deep breath next to the column of her neck. "God, your pussy smells so hot! I want to get inside it and stay there until sunrise, just slowly letting it burn my cock." He bent slightly and lifted her from the floor. A moment later her bottom rested on the same table, the marble cold against her bottom.

Lynette gasped as she looked into another full-length mirror. The single candle flame covered her in golden light as Nigel pressed her knees apart. The polished glass showed her the pink flesh of her slit and she stared at it in fascination. She had never seen her pussy before.

"You are perfection, Lynette. Stunning beyond words but not because of your body." He moved behind her and took each hand to place on the surface of the table, causing her to lean back and thrust her breasts high. Her hair spilled to the top of that table as the mirror showed her a wanton woman and her lover.

A second man's face parted from the darkness behind her to show in that reflection. One moment she saw only Nigel looking at her spread body and then there was another dark-haired man on the opposite side of her. His skin was much darker though, a deep brown that the candle glow deepened.

"This is Brenton, my half-brother."

Illegitimate floated through her brain as she looked at his dark skin again. A smile lifted her lips as she pictured Nigel's rather prim mother. If his father was anything like his son, then it was little wonder the man had sought a mistress.

Brenton watched her with intense eyes that reminded her of Nigel. He was waiting to see her reaction to his appearance and Lynette forced her body to remain just as it was. Excitement raced through her bloodstream as she considered being shared by both men.

"I think I hate you, Nigel." Brenton moved closer and stroked her arm. A shiver shook her body and he smoothed over her skin a second time.

"Now you see why I rode to see your father today." Nigel moved in front of her as he winked at her. "Brenton always tries to best me at everything. There was no way I was going to let him meet you without our engagement being discussed among the masses. Now he can't steal you away from me."

Brenton snorted behind her as he cupped both her shoulders. "Tell me you have a sister or a friend, sweet Lynette." His lips slowly lowered to her neck as he watched for her reaction in the mirror. Nigel's hands smoothed over her inner thighs. Up towards her spread slit but not close enough before he stopped and slid them back to her knees and then back up towards her center again.

Brenton's lips found her neck and he gently bit her. The sharp sting traveled down her body as Nigel's hands touched her open slit. A little moan of delight came from her as he trailed a single finger through her slit.

Nigel smiled at her as he found her clit and rubbed it. Her hips lifted towards his hand as Brenton's hands moved over her collarbones and towards her breasts. His fingers found her nipples and gently pinched them as he bit her again.

Lynette stared at Nigel before looking at the mirror to see his brother's hands on her bare breasts. Once again she was being shared but this time it felt so deeply intimate. It was an opposite from the wild indulgence of last night.

Nigel's hand left her slit and caught his cock. He stroked the ridged length before lifting his eyes to hers. "I'm going to fuck you slowly tonight, Lynette. Very, very slowly and then Brenton is going to join me inside you."

Brenton pinched her nipples as Nigel fitted the head of his cock against the opening to her pussy. He pressed it forward and her body eagerly opened for him. Her thighs spread wider as her bottom lifted from the table to allow that cock to thrust high into her pussy.

The mirror showed her Brenton's eyes watching Nigel's cock disappearing into her wet flesh. Nigel cupped her hips as he pulled free and then pressed back into her. She was so wet, his cock moved freely in and out of her pussy but Nigel kept the pace very slow as Lynette panted with growing need.

Brenton pinched her nipples again and she moaned. Low and deep, it was a sound of primitive need. Like a bitch when she went into heat. Brenton's hand trailed down her corset and right to the top of her slit. He settled one dark finger over her clit as Nigel thrust his cock back into her.

Pleasure slammed into her as her hips jerked frantically towards that finger and cock. "Yes! Oh, yes!" Nigel pulled out of her as Brenton's finger pressed down on her clit. Nigel's hands tightened on her hips as he thrust back into her pussy and Brenton pressed on her sensitive nub.

Climax made her scream as she bucked against both cock and finger. She saw the flash of teeth from Brenton as he dropped a kiss onto her shoulder. Nigel's teeth were gritted and his face a mask of tension as he pulled his cock from her body.

"When your pussy milks me I want to come so badly, but not yet, Lynette. Not yet." His words were an odd manner of warning to her. His hands pulled her forward until she felt her feet brush the floor. Nigel kept pulling until she stood.

Nigel turned her around and then pressed her forward over the table surface. She stared at Brenton as he stroked his cock. It was just an inch from her face now as Nigel smoothed his hands over her bottom.

"Spread your thighs, Lynette."

"Suck my cock."

She obeyed both men. Her feet shifting apart as she reached for Brenton's cock. He stepped forward and she licked the slit on its ruby head. There was one drop of salty fluid resting there that she licked away before taking the thing inside her mouth.

Nigel gently parted the cheeks of her bottom as she used her mouth on his brother's cock. She felt the smooth glide of lubricant being applied to her back entrance and she shivered. They were going to fuck her together. Her clit throbbed with the idea of how full two cocks would make her feel.

"Damn, she's got a wicked tongue!" Brenton caught her head and thrust his cock towards her mouth. "Suck it down good."

Nigel pressed one of his fingers into her bottom as she licked and sucked on Brenton's cock. Her bottom eagerly stretched for Nigel and she heard his chuckle as he applied more lubricant before working two and then three of his fingers into her.

Brenton's breath rasped through his teeth as his fingers tightened on her hair. He pulled her away from his cock as he shot her a look of appreciation. "Damn, I hate you, Nigel. I'd give my right eye for a lady who would suck me like this every night with the blessing of the community."

Nigel pulled his fingers from her bottom and lifted her from the table at the same time. He carried her towards the bed as Brenton followed.

"Roll over onto your knees and hands, Lynette." She giggled as she did it. Now she even looked like a bitch as well as felt like it. Nigel smoothed a hand over her bottom as he came up behind her. One hand steadied her hip as his other guided his cock towards her prepared bottom.

"Relax, Lynette." She shivered instead as the head of his cock pressed into her bottom. The skin burned as it pushed deeper but it wasn't true pain. Instead the walls of her pussy were pressed together, making her burn for another cock to stretch her there.

"Ah Lynette, I am going to fall madly in love with you before the month is out." He meant that too. It was certainly an odd time for a declaration of love but at that moment they shared a trust that let the emotions free.

Nigel pulled his cock free and then thrust slowly back into her. She moaned as the walls of her pussy screamed for the same stretching. Brenton appeared in front of her and lifted her body up until her hand twisted around his neck. Nigel pressed forward as she rose up on her knees with Nigel's cock deep in her bottom. Brenton's cock nudged her pussy and she whimpered as need breathed inside her like a living force. There was nothing that mattered but getting that second cock inside her.

Brenton thrust forward and she moaned. The sound mixed with two male grunts of approval and then she was full. Packed with both cocks, her clit exploding with pleasure and the need for friction.

"Fuck me...please."

Brenton grasped her hips as he began to work his cock. Nigel moved behind her as his cock slid smoothly in and out of her body. Lynette couldn't move or she would end up with only one cock deeply inside her. She had to stay still as they thrust and fucked her slowly, exactly as Nigel had promised they would.

She screamed as climax broke her in two. Her fingers clawed at the hard chest in front of her and she had no idea whose hands held her steady, only that she heard the harsh grunt of male satisfaction as both cocks erupted inside her.

The pleasure was so intense she floated away on its waves. Her body shook and twitched as she gripped her companions with fingers that had curled into talons.

When Lynette lifted her eyelids, she was lying on the bed. The sheets were cool against her hot skin. Nigel's hands stroked her face as he grinned into her eyes. She offered him a smile in return as she turned to find Brenton watching her from the other side of the bed. He snorted softly at Nigel and she laughed.

Family rivalry had never struck her as so much fun before!

※ ※ ※ ※ ※

It rained on their wedding day. A huge thunderstorm that shook the windows of the church and then the manor hall. Lynette giggled as her mother fussed over the weather. She herself found it quite fitting.

Her marriage was not going to be mild so there was no reason for the weather to be either!

Her groom was every inch the gentlemen and she the very charming picture of lady perfection. Their guests gossiped in the pews and drank too much champagne. Sly little smiles began coming their way as the evening grew older. Leaning towards her new husband, Lynette opened her fan to whisper behind its lace-edged surface.

"Do you know that this is the only night that everyone knows we are going upstairs to make love?"

Nigel chuckled as he stroked her thigh beneath the table. The skirting would hide his most improper action but her cheeks turned pink anyway. "I wonder what they would do if they knew we were going to fuck instead."

Lynette snapped her fan shut as she straightened in her chair. She shot Nigel a harsh glance but he simply raised an eyebrow at her in return.

A little smile broke through her temper. Well, she certainly wouldn't be bored in this marriage. Not until death parted them.

Nigel stood up and raised his champagne glass to the guests. "Ladies and gentlemen…good night."

Laughter broke through the room as he captured her hand and pulled her away from the reception. The second they reached the second floor, Lynette grabbed a handful of her skirts and petticoats to run down the hallway after her husband.

They tumbled into the master suite in a jumble of laughter and lace. Nigel tossed his hat at the waiting butler. "Good night!" He shut the door in the astonished man's face and turned to grin at Lynette.

Behind a closed door…now that was a very interesting place!

IMPROPER LESSONS

ജ

Chapter One

ഔ

It was a fine autumn morning. Brenton strolled along the sidewalk at a slow pace. Most of the ladies were looking down their noses at him and he confessed to enjoying it. Boston was milling with activity, the streets full of carts and horses. Men intent on business and ladies attending to their needs in the local mercantiles.

Even in 1886 a colored man drew attention from the upper-crust of Boston society. Maybe that was why Brenton savored it so much, he liked making sure they saw his silk brocade vest and gold pocket watch chain. He watched them through tinted, imported glasses as they noticed his fine wool overcoat and the shine on his hand-tooled boots.

There was one stark difference between him and the gentlemen passing him on the boardwalk. Brenton never wore gloves. He wore his mother's coloring proudly because he had not been born a slave.

Bastard he was, but that was his father's sin. One that Brenton refused to shoulder. He had his own to worry about but more importantly, he had a life to spend his time thinking about.

Reaching the courthouse, he climbed the stone stairs as he quickened his pace. It was time to earn his fortune.

* * * * *

Evelyn Smyth looked quite proper as she rang the bell at the Spencer Industries gate. Behind the ten-foot iron fence were some of the most modern factories in the world. Right there in Boston.

Evelyn wasn't as calm as her smooth face looked. No indeed! Excitement raced through her veins as she peered through the curling black iron to the small city within.

It truly was a miniature community. The workers lived in dormitories provided by the Spencer estate. That was not uncommon in 1886. Many large industries offered lodging as part of the employment package. Mind you, most of those companies expected their workers to work long hours, and keeping them close to the factory increased the number of work hours that the company might extract from them.

Spencer Textiles was different. Evelyn was still slightly shocked at the offer of employment she'd received.

They wanted a teacher.

Spencer Textiles intended to allow the children to go to a school that they were paying for. That was quite unheard of! Most industries worked the children as hard as the adults. Age was no matter when it came to changing bobbins on a loom. In fact, a child's smaller hands could reach into the mechanical loom easier than an adult's.

Whole families were contracted for employment right down to the five year olds. The side effect of that practice was workers locked into a generation of ignorance because they had never attended school.

Evelyn still did not know exactly what to expect. Her employment agency was one of the most esteemed in Boston, she would not have been dispatched without the Spencer company passing several interviews.

That gave her the courage to take a rail car here this morning. A schoolmarm wasn't worth anything if she did not have a good name. Reputation was everything in the society of 1886. The wealthy families who could afford a teacher like her would not tolerate even a hint of scandal attached to her name.

So, her dress buttoned exactly up to her collarbones. Her skirts were hemmed to just one inch above her polished boot toes and, of course, the top skirt was bustled in the back. A short cape was buttoned around her shoulders, hiding the trim figure her corset made. The black wool was somber and well-suited to a schoolmarm. It fell to her elbows, completing her pious appearance.

Society did like its "appearances"!

She had not been born with a silver spoon in her mouth but she did come from a good name. Her father had served as dock magistrate until his early death. Her mother had died only a year later but she had passed on her gift of knowledge to Evelyn. The Princeton agency had taken her in because her mother had taught for them.

In Boston, your name got you through gates such as these. Otherwise, she might find herself in the gutter with the dock whores.

"Good morning, Miss Smyth, delighted to see you are punctual."

Evelyn dropped a smooth curtsy to the man meeting her. She did not bob it because she was not a maid showing deference. It was a smooth motion of social respect.

"I am Mr. Bolton, overseer for Textile One. You are a bit younger than I might have envisioned."

"The Princeton agency felt I was perfect for the posting." Evelyn held her voice steady. There was another thing that society enjoyed, putting you in your place. Well, she was going to be staying and Mr. Bolton would be the one adjusting.

The chance to run her own school before she was forty was the stuff dreams were made of.

"Yes, well, here at the Spencer Industries Mr. Ashton is the final judge of everything. In truth, this is his idea. You will teach the younger students reading and math."

"Mr. Spencer does not run his own industries?" That was a bold question to ask but she needed to know exactly whom to please and in what order. She did not have the luxury of doing without her weekly pay.

"Mr. Spencer the elder is retired. Obviously, you do not understand to true scope of the Spencer holdings. Mr. Spencer the younger runs the ironworks on the north side of town. Mr. Ashton is your employer."

"Indeed." Evelyn held her chin level. A schoolmarm had to be in control at all times, even ones such as this. Unless she missed her guess, Mr. Bolton found school an intrusion into his efficiency rating.

"Yes then, the maid will show you to your school building. Sleeping quarters are in the back. Due to the fact that you come from the Princeton agency, need I make any further comments on the expected behavior of your nightly conduct?"

"Certainly not." This time Evelyn put just the right amount of righteous anger into her voice. Maintaining a pious image was essential for a schoolmarm. It was important to make sure Mr. Bolton thought she was offended by his statement.

Appearances.

* * * * *

The second the maid left, Evelyn smiled as big as a child on Christmas morning. She was walking in a dreamland! The school was its own little building that still smelled of fresh paint. It had neat rows of new desks, four across and eight deep! With two students to a desk, that made sixty-four students and there were instructions that told her there would be morning class for the younger children and the older ones would come after midday dinner.

She had done it! She was a schoolmarm! Not just a teacher but head 'marm of her own school. Oh, she would teach them! Indeed she would!

She swung around in a circle before she headed back out the door of her living quarters and turned left to the set of doors at the back of the schoolhouse. Her instructions said there was a supply closet—she was eager to see what she had to teach with—and it was nice to see the door that would provide her privacy from anyone going to that supply closet.

The doors pulled open and she stepped inside. The light was dim because thick shelves ran the length of the walls and there were only small windows along the upper part of the walls.

Evelyn stroked a thick packet of paper as she moved past it. The closet was deep. Her steps didn't make any sound because she lingered over each inch of the shelves, her eyes drinking in the stacks of books and chalk and even pencils. She practically held her breath for fear it would all dissipate like a mirage.

A sharp giggle punctured her attention. It came from the back of the closet. Looking in front of her, Evelyn saw that the closet was in fact a hallway that was converted into a storage area by placing doors on either end. That was why it was so long.

The schoolhouse wasn't standing alone, she just had not seen the corridor that connected it to the block of dormitories because it was attached to the back of the school building. Once the snow flew, it would be much better for the children to enter the school through the supply corridor.

"Who needs his cock sucked?"

Her eyes bulged as she slapped a hand over her mouth She had never once heard that word spoken out loud.

"I've work to do, Laura."

"Oh, now is that any way to start the day? Your cock swollen behind them trousers? Want to fuck me instead?"

Evelyn looked behind her but she was alone, the set of doors she'd entered the stockroom through had fallen closed behind her. Light came in through the small windows above the shelves. A hard male groan came through the closed doors in front of her as she heard odd wet sounds. Like a child eating his soup too quickly.

Were they...ah...mating? Is that what it sounded like? Temptation nagged at her to peek through the wood slats. Just a tiny glance so that she would know what a man and woman did together. Was it really so wrong to know?

"Suck it, Laura."

Suck what? Evelyn couldn't quite believe that anyone would actually place their mouth onto a man's genitals. For what reason? Her foot lifted from the floor before she thought to stop it. One moment later, she could see through the boards that made up one side of the door.

Evelyn bit into her gloved hand at the sight. A huge man was leaning against a desk. His powerful legs spread to brace against the floor. Kneeling between his legs was a woman and in her hands was...sweet mercy!

A cock.

That thing that mothers whispered about to their daughters on their wedding nights. That flesh that good girls were warned to never think about lest they become fallen women. It sprang up from the man's open fly some good eight inches. The head was the size of a small plum and Laura opened her mouth and sucked it. Those little wet sounds came from her as she twisted her head and pulled the plum-sized head into her mouth.

"Use your tongue." The man grasped a handful of her hair and pushed her head towards his cock. More of the dark length entered her mouth and she moaned. Not with pain but it sounded like she was enjoying her cock-sucking.

Evelyn should have left. It was pure insanity to watch something like this but her blood raced through her veins and she could not pull her eyes from the couple.

It was so forbidden yet she craved the sight of it.

"Enough." The man pulled Laura away from his cock as his breath hissed through his gritted teeth. "Stand up and lean over the desk. I'll give you that fucking you asked for."

Laura giggled like a schoolgirl as she stood up. She grabbed two handfuls of her skirts and pulled them all the way to her waist. She turned and lay over the desk with her bottom bare. She wore no knickers to get in the way as she spread her legs apart, showing off the deep pink of her sex.

"You've got a hot pussy, Laura. I don't even mind that you share it." The woman gasped and tried to rise from the desk surface. The man pushed her down with one hand as his other reached for a small item in his vest pocket. He opened the package and then used both his hands to roll a thin sheath over his cock. He worked it all the way to the base where two sacs hung beneath his staff. One large hand gripped Laura's hip as his other hand grasped the thick cock and guided the head to her spread body.

He shoved forward and Laura moaned again as his cock disappeared into her body. "Did you think I didn't know, Laura?" He pulled his cock out and then pushed it back into her. "I'm no fool."

His body moved back and forth but he kept one hand around the very base of his cock to keep the protective sheath in place. His cock would appear and then disappear as he thrust it into her body. Laura gasped and moaned like she couldn't contain her cries. "You're a good fuck but you don't much care whose cock is stretching your pussy."

"Brenton, don't be mad!"

He chuckled in response and pulled out of her body. He reached for her hip and rolled her over. Laura lifted one of her legs right over his head as she spread her thighs on that desktop. Brenton stroked a finger through her spread sex before shoving his cock deeply into her.

"Fucking you has been fun, Laura, but I'll not risk getting the pox, so this is your last ride from me."

Laura sobbed but her hips lifted in time with Brenton's thrusts. Her head thrashed on the desktop as she clawed at his forearms. "Just like that, hmm?"

"Yes, Brenton...harder!" Laura thrashed like a wild creature as she moaned deep and long. The man riding her grunted before he grabbed her hips and shoved his entire length deep into her. They froze for a lingering moment before he pulled his cock free and pulled the sheath from it. The ruby head was glistening with moisture as he reached for a handkerchief to dry it with. The used sheath was crumpled up as he tossed the dirty linen away and began to button his trousers.

"Now, don't cling. It's been fun but you were no virgin when I first fucked you, Laura. Be a good girl and see if you can't get Rudy Yeoman to take you to church for a wedding."

Evelyn was amazed to see Laura push herself off the desk and grin at her ex-lover. She began fixing her clothing and hair as she reached for his buttoned fly. Her fingers stroked the hidden cock one more time. "Oh, you're right, but you can't blame a gal for wanting a taste of that cock. It's the biggest I ever had. That's your colored blood there. I hear colored men have the biggest cocks around."

* * * * *

She was going to hell.

Evelyn was still hearing the echo of their...*fucking* in her head as she made her way back to her living quarters. There was a set of doors that would give her privacy to the small apartment and she quickly shut them and turned the lock.

She had just watched them! It defied her ability to understand her own brain. Something had risen from inside her and insisted that she see what the forbidden looked like.

But that wasn't what truly alarmed her.

Her body had responded. Right then her blood moved quickly through her veins. Her nipples had actually tingled for some odd reason and deep in her belly she felt a pulse that she had never once felt in all of her twenty-two years of life.

Oh my...was she soiled now? Beyond redemption?

Evelyn smiled a little. No, she was not that bad off. She knew what stealing was too, but that did not make her a thief.

The little pulse between her legs turned into an ache. Such an odd response to find in her own flesh. It was almost like she might enjoy being the one on that desk. She actually giggled because it was such a foreign idea! Mating was for the marriage bed and only as a duty. Well-bred ladies did not enjoy the carnal attentions of their husbands but endured it for the sake of producing a family.

To crave what she had just witnessed branded her a lesser creature than the well-bred ladies of upper society.

But then, appearances often conflicted with the emotions a person was expected to contain beneath the polished exterior.

* * * * *

"You are a rather pleasant surprise."

The voice was deep and very masculine. Evelyn turned around and gasped. It was a tiny sound but the man in front of her heard it. His chocolate-colored eyes flashed but not with outrage. It appeared that he enjoyed startling her.

It was *him*.

She struggled to keep her eyes on his face. She had the insane urge to look at his fly. Clinging tightly to her composure, Evelyn noted the light brown of his skin. Yes, he was a colored man but still a very handsome one.

His shoulders were large and they complemented his towering height. Her head only came to his shoulder when she was used to being almost equal with most men. His jaw was square but undeniably masculine.

His fine attire spoke of wealth that she only dreamed of. His silk brocade vest easily worth a week of her pay. There was only one man who would enter the schoolroom with that kind of money. Her eyes tried to bulge as she absorbed the truth that she had actually spied on her employer during his…escapades.

"Good afternoon, Mr. Ashton."

Brenton was fascinated with his new teacher. Maybe it was the idea of expecting to find a short little man with glasses perched on the end of his nose that made the vision in front of him so very delectable. That did the lady an injustice, though.

She was well-figured and stood rather tall for a woman. Her waist was pulled in by a corset but the bosom contained with whalebone and steel looked plump and inviting. His cock gave a twitch as his mind considered her chest again. Her bottom must be plump and sassy too.

His lips rose in a slow smile. His new schoolmarm wouldn't take kindly to his ideas about what hid under her skirts but that didn't halt the surge of heat filling his cock. Delicate ladies were quite the fashion but he enjoyed a woman with a good fanny. The kind a man could hold on to when he rode her.

"I wanted to make certain you have everything you desire."

His words took her mind where it did not belong. Evelyn scolded her lapse of mental control. Mr. Ashton was speaking of his school, not her misplaced spying! He held not a clue that she had witnessed his morning romp and was not offering her a similar invitation.

Besides, that sort of idea would land Evelyn in ruin. Oh yes, a man like this one had many women. Society might frown on it but he wouldn't be the one tarred with shame. No, it would be her name sullied about as a slut. He did not make honest women of his lovers. She had heard it with her own ears.

"The school is so much more than I dared hope for. You are a generous man."

She dropped him a little curtsy and that made Brenton frown. Proper conduct wasn't what his cock twitched for from her. The surge of need was completely unexpected. He enjoyed women but his body had never demanded one before.

"My father believes in education. Happy workers are loyal ones."

Oh my... Evelyn didn't gasp this time, instead her breath froze in her lungs. The level of boldness astonished her. It also excited her. She was wicked to enjoy his brassy statement. Speaking out plainly of being illegitimate like it was a benign topic suitable for a schoolroom.

"I believe you are blushing." He chuckled as he took a few more steps into the room. "Why? Because I admit to being a bastard? That was my parents' sin. I do assure you, Evelyn, I save my repenting for my own deviations from the prim and proper."

"I'm certain you do." A wicked image of his large cock moved through her thoughts as she heard the echo of Laura's moans. Brenton Ashton did have his own sins to account for.

One dark eyebrow rose as he moved in a slow circle around her. His eyes very deliberately dropped down her body in a lingering inspection of her form. The fact that every employer she had ever had did the same thing did not stop her cheeks from burning even hotter. This man was not taking notice of how correct her dress was, he was looking at the curves beneath the fabric.

Stop it, Eve!

She was going straight to hell. Letting temptation guide her this morning had pulled her into the flames of damnation. Now, her thoughts tumbled into ideas of the flesh at a snap of the fingers!

Or in this case, being face-to-face with a man whose naked cock she had viewed. It gave the term "awkward" a new meaning.

His fingers stroked her flaming cheek and she jumped. "Mr. Ashton." Eve slapped a hand over her mouth because her words didn't sound as outraged as they should. There was breathlessness edging them that betrayed the excitement his touch ignited. Her composure was deserting her as Brenton Ashton stepped closer.

"Yes? Should I ignore that scarlet rush of blood in your cheeks?" He was behaving like a bully. If he didn't curb his need to rattle her composure, he just might find himself needing another schoolmarm before sunset.

But that didn't make him feel guilty. His cock was so hard it bordered on pain. Standing even three steps from her was too far.

"Indeed you should."

The man folded his arms across his chest and stared at her. It was the honest truth that Evelyn watched his eyes because she could truly see a battle being fought there. There was a part of her that filled with pride for having attracted this much attention from him. Honestly, she could not remember eliciting anything close to this from another gentleman.

But then Mr. Ashton wasn't in fact a true gentleman. His clothing hid a base nature that he embraced. No gentleman would be so bold with a schoolmarm. Maybe this manner of behavior was appropriate for women like Laura, who spread their thighs whenever the urge took them. That was what Evelyn had been taught to recognize in the people around her, some were better-blooded than others. Answering the body's craving to mate was common, it placed you in the same category as a bitch that went into heat each season.

A shiver shook her spine. Brenton would do things to her that she had only heard whispers about. If she was bold enough to cast her fortunes to the winds, this man would be the lover to indulge her body with. She sensed the raw power in him and could almost swear she smelled how aggressive he was.

No, keeping up her appearances wouldn't allow her to do something so completely...impulsive. It simply was not done, and risking her newfound position was too high a price to put on mere back hallway whispers. Rumors had a very disappointing way of turning out to be little more than bluster, built on a small fact and gossiped into a larger than life fantasy.

Evelyn forgot that while she watched him. Brenton was considering her in return. The flame in his eyes brightened as her eyes slipped to his shoulders before she pulled them back to his face. His pleasant expression was missing as he shot a warning straight into her eyes.

He suddenly moved and Evelyn jumped before her brain absorbed the fact that he was walking away from her. She sucked in a large breath just before Brenton very precisely turned the lock on the door.

Chapter Two

ဆ

The harsh metal sound bounced off the walls as her heart tripled its pace. Brenton turned around and considered her reaction.

"I should ignore that blush, but I wonder if that is what either of us would enjoy the most."

His words were full of presumption. Heat flared up in her belly but her brain warned her to resist. Her eyes fell on the bolt he'd just turned and the hallway that connected to his own office.

"Truly, sir! I find your actions rather suspect. Did you have my living quarters placed in connection with your office to make your visits easier to accomplish? If so, you have greatly misjudged my character."

Brenton should have left. Her prim-looking hair and high-collared blouse fit her words perfectly, casting him into the role of villain. But there was something in her tone that held his attention. It was the ring of anger instead of outrage that made his cock twitch again. It was the idea that he thought she was easy that bothered her. Not the prospect of his attention as her proper image should have led him to believe.

"The schoolhouse is connected to my office because there are far too many fathers and overseers here who believe a child can do just as well in this world without the knowledge to read." Brenton held up one thick finger. "I have the roster and each and every single child will be counted by me on their way to this school. Would you like to know why, Evelyn? Because my own mother was born a slave. Forbidden by law to learn to read. I refuse to see greed take the place of slave laws in keeping children of any color ignorant."

Her eyes went wide but her mouth softened and it hit him straight in the heart. Having principles might be a good thing for a man but finding someone who truly understood him was as rare as striking gold. Evelyn's eyes shimmered with unshed tears as she nodded her head.

"Forgive me, sir, I have been extremely rude."

"Not really, I was far too forward but I am not apologizing." He closed the distance between them and did not stop until he was a mere two steps from her. "I enjoyed touching you, Evelyn, and I am not sorry I did it. Improper or not." Brenton took that last step and her nostrils filled completely with his warm male scent. There was no chance of controlling her response. The heat in her belly shot up in flames that stroked her breasts and down to the most forbidden parts of her sex.

"I touched you because I wanted to." His ungloved hand cupped her chin as his lips landed on hers. His other hand caught a handful of her skirt, pinning her in place as his mouth delivered a hard kiss. He pushed her lips open, angling his head to deepen the contact.

Evelyn had never been kissed like this. Proper soft compressions on the cheek but nothing like the full press of his hot mouth. His tongue thrust down into her mouth as she gasped. It was blatantly raw, his tongue thrusting into her body just like his cock could thrust into her.

It was so forbidden but her hand rose and landed on his chest as she lost the battle to remain away from him. She craved a harder embrace where the shape of his body would no longer be just something her eyes showed her. Evelyn wanted to touch and stroke the shoulders that impressed her so much.

"Kiss me back." Brenton's voice was harsh with demand. She actually felt the walls of her passage ache in response to the sound of his breath rasping next to her ear.

"I don't know…um…I've never…"

His hand snaked around her waist and pulled her against his body. He released her chin and slid his fingers into her neat bun at the nape of her neck. His fingers held her head as Brenton tipped her face up towards his.

"Use your tongue the way I do. Stroke my tongue with yours and open your mouth wide so they can mingle inside yours." His eyes glowed with hunger as he leaned down to press his mouth against hers. There was no asking, his kiss was hard and pressed her mouth to yield.

His tongue swept deeply in towards hers as pleasure shot down her spine. Her breasts tingled as the nipples drew into tight little buttons. His tongue stroked hers and she did the same in return. A harsh grunt hit her ears and she swore it was one of deep satisfaction. It was such a primitive sound but she absorbed it with a portion of her brain that was just as primal.

"God, you taste good." Brenton trailed his lips over her cheek to her jaw. The tightly buttoned collar of her blouse bothered him. He itched to rip it and expose her tender skin. He still held her head and he pulled it back farther as he popped the first button open. He leaned forward and licked the skin as she shivered in his arms.

Brenton enjoyed that telltale sign from her body. Lurking inside his prim little schoolmarm was a woman. He could smell her despite the layers of fabric containing the soft skin. A craving grew in his cock to brand her, thrust deep into her body and fill her with his seed.

Evelyn was helpless in his arms. The embrace was so solid but not painful. The level of control amazed her but she sensed it could tighten in a flash if she resisted.

The horrible truth was, she did not want to struggle away from him. Her body shook with delight as another of her buttons separated and his mouth pressed against that freed skin. Heat grew as it was carried by her blood. Every inch of her skin cried out for freedom as her passage began to throb with the same frantic beat as her heart. The hand on her waist moved and dived between the flounces of her bustle to boldly cup one side of her bottom. Her belly was pressed up against his body and she felt the hard shape of his cock beneath his trousers.

The clear reality of what he wanted to do with that cock sobered her. Evelyn twisted violently away from the temptation and rolled right over her desk. Brenton let her hair go or it would have been ripped from her head. A long hank of the dark strands cascaded over her shoulder, the pins clattering to the desktop. His eyes blazed their fury at her as she fought off the lamenting of her own body to fling herself back into his arms. "I cannot!"

"Why not?" Brenton was clinging to control. She sensed it and there was part of her that wanted to watch that product of society snap as the animal raged forward.

"I want this job, this school." It was her last stand against the tide of heat sweeping through her. Every tiny hair covering her skin was stiff. Places she had never felt clamoring for attention suddenly were. Temptation never called so loudly before. Her legs shook beneath her skirt as she fought the desire to lower her eyes to his fly. Her body craved to be next to that cock, her fingertips eagerly demanding to stroke it and discover what it felt like.

He reached over the desk and stroked her face as he nodded. "I might want to fuck you, Evelyn, but that doesn't mean I'd ruin your name."

"It's the same thing."

"No, it isn't, not to me." He considered her eyes with a dark intensity that made her shiver again. He saw the involuntary motion and frowned. A moment later, Brenton moved towards the locked door but turned before twisting the bolt. "This is far from over. But you're right about one thing, I need to make sure our fucking stays between us."

That metal click hit her ears and then Brenton was gone. Evelyn stared at the unlatched door in numb shock until a breeze flowed through the open panel and hit that last, lingering kiss on her neck.

She flew across the room and turned the bolt. Turning on her heel, she went into the dressing room to confront a reflection that froze her in her tracks.

That could not be her!

Her lips were shiny from his kiss. Her cheeks still red from the blood speeding along her limbs because her heart was pounding. Not just a fast beat but deep compressions that she could feel all the way through her torso.

Her corset bit into her lungs as they struggled for more breath. In truth, she detested her layers of clothing right then. Her skin demanded freedom. Tucked into the hard cotton of her stays were nipples that were still tight little buttons. They throbbed and begged for the same hot kiss that her neck had sampled.

Was this how insanity took hold of the mind?

The woman staring back at her was foreign because she looked sensual. Banished was the prim schoolmarm. In her place, were dislodged hairpins and open buttons. Deep in her passage she could feel the wet slide of fluid, it even spilled onto the top of her thighs making her drawers stick to them.

Never once had she felt such burning need to sin. Her passage was craving the hard thrust of Brenton's cock, and knowing it was wrong did not change it.

Yet, was it so wrong? Evelyn picked up her hairbrush and began to smooth her hair into a neat hank that could once again be pinned to the back of her head. Right then, there was no one to judge her. Brenton had felt the same raging desire as she, in many ways they had fed off each other. Exciting the other and driving the need deeper.

All appearances aside, did it really matter when the door was firmly bolted, if she fed that craving? Dare she allow Brenton to do what he said he would? She scoffed at her thought. Honestly, the man had declared it bluntly as if he thought she might click her boot heels together like a soldier and say "Yes, Sir".

Fuck her. Really, she had never heard that word either, at least not in relation to her own body. Society had all sorts of delicate ways to talk about the duties of a wife but "fuck" wasn't spoken to any woman who ranked above a dock hussy.

Maybe a hussy was more honest than she was.

Evelyn stared at her face as she pushed her hairpins into place. Each one felt like it was going through her scalp instead of just hair. Her flesh fought being pressed back into containment. So that made her more the sinner than a dockside hussy. The prim schoolmarm was a deception that she was willingly forcing her body to don.

At least the hussy was honest—damn society and its appearances!

Maybe she should more justifiably damn Brenton. The scriptures blamed Eve for tempting Adam but today it was the male who had introduced her to the bit of temptation.

* * * * *

"Tea for you, Miss Smyth."

Evelyn turned from her blackboard and stared at the maid. The girl dropped a curtsy as she placed a tea service tray on the teacher's desk at the front of the schoolroom. The girl left a second later leaving Evelyn rolling her piece of chalk between her fingers as she contemplated the steam rising from the spout of the pot.

She was not accustomed to being served. She knew it was teatime but higher servants in a home had to report to the kitchen if they wanted to enjoy the afternoon tradition.

A small violet card sat on the tray. Placing her chalk on the holding tray beneath the blackboard, she stepped towards the tea. Obviously, she was being served today as a welcome and should not expect service henceforth. Evelyn turned the little envelope over to find it wax-sealed and the Ashton signet pressed into the red wax. The red dye in that sealing wax would stain the parchment of the envelope giving absolute evidence of any tampering. The masculine writing on the inside card gave her pause as she lifted it from the envelope to read the message.

This blend is known for keeping the figure slim in spite of any passionate pursuits a lady might harbor. I have it on good word that it does its job well. Drink it each day. Brenton.

Indeed! The utter nerve of that man! Oh, she knew what the tea was! Had heard the rumor of its amazing ability to keep a family from growing beyond the parents' abilities to provide. Yes, she was gently bred, but even among good names the realities of penny and dollar must be considered. The wealthy could afford to raise their lady daughters to never hear of such a thing as birth prevention but she had not been born on a lofty estate where endless babes were no hardship.

Somehow, it had never crossed her mind that the tea could be employed to prevent an illegitimate child from coming into the world. Mind you, that was mostly due to the fact that her thoughts centered around making certain that men did not view her as desirable. Plain, prim, proper…those were the words that Evelyn wanted to come to mind when she was seen, not ideas of what her nipples looked like or how her lips tasted.

A cloth bag was sitting on the tray and it was full of dry tea. Lifting it to her nose, Evelyn inhaled the pungent scent. The brew was quite bitter and she tipped the lid of the pot back to discover only hot water inside.

Brenton's parting words cut through her anger. Evelyn would wager money that the maid had no idea the teapot contained only hot water. The servant had been given a task and while she might wonder, she would never know for sure.

Temptation renewed its grip on her body. A soft pulse began in her sex as she looked at the thin taper of steam coming from the water. Right or wrong she could do as she pleased with the appearance of the bag of tea. No one would know, how could they if her belly did not swell with child?

The desks suddenly caught her eye as did the door the maid had entered through. She picked up the tray and moved towards her living quarters. She kicked the door shut and placed the tea service on her little parlor table before moving quickly back to turn the bolt.

Evelyn stared at the bolt as she listened to Brenton's words again in her memory. If no one knew, if no one could see, was yielding to the flesh wrong?

Oh, it was wicked temptation!

At twenty-two and a schoolmarm, her chances to marry were dwindling. Few men wanted a wife in a position higher than their own and there were not many servants who ranked above the schoolmarm. Especially here, where Evelyn answered only to the head employer. True, there were men in Boston she might marry if she caught their eye, but there would be few opportunities to leave Spencer Textiles.

That was further ensured by the little apartment she stood in right then. There was a parlor and a small kitchen that shared one room. A doorway led to her bedroom that had a bathroom attached to it. There was even a tub with its own pump. She need only heat a kettle and carry it to the tub for bathing. The porcelain-coated slipper tub sat on four brass feet and had a drain at the bottom that released the used water to the main city sewer. It was the height of modern conveniences. It was actually better than she might have afforded to furnish for herself if she took a position in the city schools.

The apartment was quite frankly a reflection of how important learning was to Brenton. Her heart gave a twist, Evelyn just couldn't help it. Brenton's dedication to learning endeared him to her. Deep inside that man was a core of integrity. It was rare in many humans. So often greed and selfishness filled people so full of their own ego, there was no room for the plight of others.

After all, it was much simpler to point a finger in judgment than to offer your hand in assistance.

That did not mean she would be granting Brenton any further liberties with her person.

Her sex trembled in response as she looked back at the tea. Biting her lower lip she considered the way she had lost all manner of control right here in her parlor. The locked door somehow attributing to her fall from grace by granting her permission to indulge because there was no one to judge her.

Except Brenton.

It would very simple for the employer to judge her harshly for wanton behavior. Mind you, the warnings her mother had given her said he should be pressing her to yield or lose her position. Instead, Brenton had sent her the tea to help her conceal any affair they might have.

Yet, he had left her that afternoon. Stepping forward, Evelyn measured out a serving of the tea and placed it in the pot to brew. It would have been so simple to press her for more that morning, her own body would have helped him gain her surrender.

She might not like it but that did not mean she should ignore a fact that might rise up to confront her again. A bit of precaution was certainly not misplaced given her lapse of control in Brenton's arms.

Evelyn wrinkled her nose as she took the first sip. Sweet Mary, it was noxious! But keeping up appearances was often taxing on the whims.

Oh, she was wicked!

And Brenton was Satan, temptation incarnate. The only true question left in her thoughts was which torment she might rather be left holding. The soft throb of unsatisfied hunger that gripped her body now or the burden of knowing she had indulged her primitive nature when everything in her society dictated that she should cling to her morality.

Evelyn lifted the tea to her lips again. Whatever her choice, she would not brand a child with her decision.

Chapter Three

The supper whistle blew, startling Evelyn from her lesson plans. She firmly closed her books and went to fetch her cape from the hook in the doorway. Meals were also served in dormitory style. Each family couldn't have fires going in their living spaces all throughout the large dormitories. The risk of fire would be enormous.

So there was an eating hall with a kitchen that serviced the workforce. Picking up her feet, she hurried to follow the streams of workers into the eating hall. The meal would be put down and if you dawdled, you would take an empty belly to bed.

Her living quarters were luxury compared to the people she joined in the hall. She even had a small stove that could be used for cooking, but at present there were no food supplies in her cupboards. Laying in a meager supply of dry stock might be a wise idea though. It always paid to be ready to provide for yourself.

"Evening, Miss Smyth."

"Pleasure to have you with here, Miss Smyth."

Pleasant greetings and smiles met her before she even made it into the hall. Children ran past as they joined their parents, and mothers turned those little ones to look at her. They smiled huge grins at her, most of them missing teeth, as they all shuffled into the hall.

A smile lifted her lips as she was greeted by even more workers. The air was full of laughter and good-natured conversation. While their clothing sported the soil stains of a hard day's labor, these people lacked the beaten expressions that often went with working for large textile companies. They had risen at daybreak and still had energy to jest as they filed onto the long benches that served as seating.

Large rounds of bread were already on the tables and there were plenty. Black cast-iron spider pots were steaming on the end of each ten-foot-long table. One person stood to serve the main stew with a ladle as the workers passed their bowls up and the filled ones back down to the opposite end.

As she got closer, Evelyn saw the small pots of jam sat out to eat with the bread. Bowls of vegetables were present and corn-battered fish. It was a generous supper. Far better than most of these people could have provided for their own children. It was one of the reasons the industries had a constant supply of workers willing to leave their tiny farms in favor of living in the dormitory. A failed crop did not translate into starvation during the winter.

"Miss Smyth, please join us at the head table."

Brenton's voice startled her with its rich formality. Plenty of eyes watched him as he offered her a polite bow and extended his hand towards a table at the top of the room. Mr. Bolton was watching her from his seat with ten other overseers.

"Thank you, Mr. Ashton. I apologize for being tardy." One corner of Brenton's mouth twitched up as she passed and took a seat. Evelyn looked at the fare resting on the table and found it to be exactly the same as the other tables. The only difference was that they had chairs instead of plank benches.

Brenton sat at the head of the table and took a bowl that was passed to him. That action endeared him to her further. Easily he could have had a butler service his supper at a finer table set with china and linen but Brenton ate with his workers, even shared the same fare.

"So, you're our schoolmarm. Indeed, I believe the children have stood in the yard watching that schoolhouse being built." One of the overseers shot her a wink with a grey eyebrow. "You'll find them eager for lessons, Miss Smyth."

"I will be delighted to have them."

The table erupted with tales of how each man had come by his own schooling. Laughter filled the hall from the other tables as Brenton watched her from his spot across the table. There was nothing in his manner that hinted at their afternoon lapse of control. His manners were polished and perfect as he made appropriate comments that never once bordered on anything personal.

Oh, but she did not need him to help along her imagination. Dark little visions of their moments together insisted on floating through her mind as she broke off a chunk of bread. Dipping into the jam allowed her mind to wander to that moment when Brenton had pressed her to his body and that cock made itself known. Her mind offered up a perfect recollection of what it looked like. Thick and long, truly Evelyn might have questioned if it could fit into a woman except she had watched Laura take it all and enjoy it.

This was absurd! It was little wonder that mothers warned their daughters to steer well clear of men. One kiss and you were hooked like a fish! Her body was ceding control like a weed spreading its seeds through a fine garden, choking the delicate flowers with deep, twisting roots. Meanwhile she twisted and flopped like a fish being pulled from the water on its way to Brenton's net and his supper plate.

Right then his eyes met hers across the table and she caught a hint of a flame before he turned his attention to the man next to him. Evelyn was relieved to notice that the meal was nearing its end now. Workers were standing up to begin clearing the tables and wash dishes before too much oil was burned in the lamps lighting the hall.

Brenton stood up and tossed his napkin aside. "Goodnight, lady and gentlemen. Work waits for no man, even me." There was a round of chuckles as other overseers took their employer's cue and made their own excuses.

Evelyn stood up, but she turned to find a row of mothers all waiting for her attention. They clasped young children by

131

the wrist and told them to stand straight. The hope glowing on their faces humbled her. Her heart gave that odd twist again as she looked at the community Brenton had built of his textile industry. It was a marvel among pitiful examples where other textile owners pounded their workers into hopeless drones.

Evelyn moved forward to begin learning her students' names. Brenton might be a raw man but he was certainly a good one at heart.

* * * * *

Her heart was bursting as she made her way to her school. The stars cast enough light to see by as Evelyn hurried across the courtyard. The night had descended with a bitter edge and a brisk wind. Her little cape was no match for the autumn chill. She would have to ask what kind of cloth Spencer Industries produced and see if they sold their imperfect bolts to their employees. A thick winter cape sounded very nice, as did a new flannel petticoat.

Evelyn locked the main schoolhouse door solidly behind her as she moved through the center aisle of desks. There were gas jet lamps outside the windows that allowed her to navigate but she would be wise to take a candle lantern with her to supper henceforth.

There was a yellow glow bleeding into the darkness as she neared the doorway to her living apartment. A single candle burned on the parlor table, its light fending off complete blackness because the window drapes were thick and prevented the gas lamps from spilling any light into her apartment.

"I thought you might have decided to tuck tail and run."

Brenton's voice didn't startle her. Somehow, Evelyn knew he was the one who had lit the candle. He formed from the darkness as her heart accelerated, but not in fear—oh no—it was far worse than that emotion. Excitement filled her blood as heat flickered to life in her belly and breasts like coals did at the touch of tinder.

"I'm quite delighted to see you didn't scurry back to your Princeton agency to blacken my name."

A tiny smile lifted her lips, in truth, she might very well have done so. Certainly there were a great many who would scold her for not stomping away with outrage dripping from their mouths.

Brenton moved past her and turned the bolt. He watched her as he did it. His square cut jaw tight as his eyes considered her intensely. "Why are you still here, Eve?"

"I deal with my own confrontations, thank you. Besides, I believe it would have been most simple for you to denounce me as well. So, we are currently even as I see it."

He still could denounce her. Because she was there, he might have his way and then cast her into the street and soil her name with the Princeton agency. As rich as Brenton was, they might not even ask her opinion on the matter, instead convict her on Brenton's testimony alone. After all, there were a great many people who viewed the golden rule as a good reason to side with whoever had the most gold.

Still, she did not believe he would do such a thing. Sending her that bag of tea had clearly shown her that he meant his words about keeping their *relationship* between only them. His actions at dinner clearly showed that he would keep their rather flammable reaction to each other behind a locked door.

Trust was such a dangerous thing to grant him. Evelyn wasn't even sure just why the emotion persisted. Brenton was still quite dangerous, yet there wasn't even the shadow of fear lurking in her heart that he would ruin her name. This man intended to deal with her personally. The certainty of it burned in his eyes and sent a shudder down her spine.

Brenton stepped towards her on silent feet. The manner in which he moved struck her as more of a prowl than a stride. She felt his attention on her like the keen glare of a predator.

"What happens between a man and a woman shouldn't be anyone's concern as long as they aren't hurting each other." Brenton touched her cheek and her breath caught in a little rasp. "I wanted to touch you, so I did." He stroked over her chin and down her neck as she leaned her head back just a bit to let him touch her bare skin. He found the button that held her cape closed and separated it. The black wool fluttered away as he tossed it across the room.

Brenton closed his eyes as her scent rose to his nose. She smelled too good for some unknown reason. While he enjoyed a freshly bathed woman, this was something different. It went deeper into his brain, into a core that was as primitive as the first human. His blood surged with the scent as his cock stiffened with the need to take. The urge went beyond the desire to fuck. What he wanted was to brand her, claim her body with his, marking it as his territory.

"This is insanity," Evelyn moaned as she listened to her blouse buttons parting. The thing about it that shocked her the most was the growing desire to have the garment torn from her body. Indeed, a touch of violence sounded exciting as she suffered through the time it took for Brenton to reach her waist.

"That's because someone told you to think like that." Her blouse was open and Brenton parted it with his hands. She felt those warm hands move over her shoulders as he pushed her blouse down her arm. "The age of man is so worried about higher thinking, they overlook the pure reaction of male to female." Her blouse joined her cape as his eyes moved over the swells of her breasts. Her corset pushed the two mounds of flesh up and Brenton's lips parted to show her an even row of teeth.

"Why in the hell does it matter if we enjoy touching each other?" Brenton stroked a finger over her bare breast above her corset and pleasure shot through her skin and raced towards her spine. Her body was acutely aware of his warm fingertip as it glided over her flesh. Little goose bumps rose on the soft skin and the throb in her passage deepened as she felt the slide of fluid once again on the top of her thighs.

But his touch was not enough. Evelyn lifted her hand and laid it on his chest. Beneath his shirt was hard muscle that she craved to stroke. She hesitated as she moved over the iron-pressed cotton because it had never crossed her mind that she might be the one touching. Good girls were taught to lie still as their husbands performed their duty.

Evelyn was certain she would go mad if she had to be touched and not touch in return. Right then her body was erupting with urges to move and press towards Brenton. Reach for what she wanted and indulge her whims.

"I do enjoy it."

Evelyn spoke in a whisper but it was as loud as an explosion to Brenton. This wasn't a woman given to lifting her skirts lightly. Evelyn didn't indulge her pussy in order to escape the harsher edges of her life. Desire sparkled in her eyes and it was more than the need to fuck. She wanted him, everything about him deepened the glow in her eyes. It actually humbled him to see that approval simmering in her dark eyes. If it didn't pack such a punch as it hit his gut, he would have laughed. Needing a woman's approval had never been one of his plans, yet tonight he noticed just how precious it was coming from Evelyn.

Brenton pulled his shirt open with one huge wrench of his hands. Evelyn gasped at the surge of raw power. Excitement stabbed into her passage as she viewed his chest. It was magnificent, she wasn't certain just how to explain why she found the hard male nipples attractive, yet she did. Her hands reached for his skin and he gasped as she slid her fingers through the tightly curled hair covering his chest. She found the smooth skin beneath that dark hair but approved of the harsher rasp of the hair too. Evelyn realized that she did not want Brenton to be soft, she craved his strength.

A hard moan shook his chest as she moved down to his belly. Knowing his cock was contained in his trousers made her bold. She was impatient to discover what it felt like, what did that oh-so forbidden part of the male animal *feel* like when you wrapped your fingers around it.

Brenton's hands appeared on his waistband as they made efficient work of the fastenings. As he spread his fly open like a dare for her hands, Evelyn looked up to find his eyes watching her. "Go on, Eve, pull my cock out."

His words were blunt but they excited her with their hard edge. It was a cock and Evelyn suddenly didn't want Brenton to use any other word for his genitals. She craved his strength and along with that went blunt language.

"I shall." She reached into his fly and found the hard staff. The skin was so hot she shivered as she grasped it and lifted it through the opening. Evelyn dropped her gaze to it and closed her grip around it. The head was the size of a plum and it had a thick ridge around its crown. A slit marked the center of the top and a tiny drop of fluid shimmered there.

"That's it, baby, learn it, stroke it," Brenton growled at her as he tried to hang on to his control. Her little fingers moved down his cock and then back up it to the slit. She rubbed just her thumb through the eye and then carried the first drop of cum to the underside of the head.

His orders sent another wave of delight through her. Would Brenton order her to suck his cock? She shook slightly as she thought about being on her knees in front of him. A wicked desire to listen to him moan in pleasure filled her.

Could she be the aggressor here? In the moments they were locked away from the society that would brand them gutter filth for their indulgencies. Dare she steal a moment of control over a man and listen to him enjoy it?

"I saw you with Laura." Evelyn stroked his cock as Brenton jerked with surprise. He shook his head and glared at her. Evelyn smiled at his astonishment. "I walked into the supply hallway and there you were with this...cock," her hand closed around his cock, "out for my eyes to see."

Brenton chuckled as he reached forward and dipped his fingers into her corset. Her fingers fumbled as he found her nipples and lifted them from her stays. He rolled the twin little buttons between his thumbs and fingers as she lost control of his cock and he pressed her back until her legs hit the parlor table. It was a sturdy four-legged one and held her as Brenton pressed against her.

"Damn closet wasn't there last month." His mouth landed on hers as he rolled her nipples again. He pushed her lips apart and his tongue swept in to mingle with hers. Evelyn clung to his shoulders as his kiss continued to taste her. Her confession had empowered someone all right—Brenton wasn't bound by the same tight control any longer. Yet she had willingly baited him and satisfaction surged through her as he laid a row of hard kisses down her neck.

Right where her shoulder and neck met, he bit her. It was a sharp sting that he licked away with the tip of his tongue. Her nipples begged for the same hot kiss as they hung over the top of her corset. Brenton's head dipped towards them as one of his arms slid around her waist. He bent her over that arm and then sucked her right nipple into his mouth.

Her cry bounced off the far wall but there was no way to contain it. That nipple was connected in a solid current to her passage. Right at the top of her sex some unknown part of her body demanded attention. Evelyn had no idea what it was, it wasn't the deep passage that Laura had called her pussy. No, this was hidden in the folds that protected that sheath.

"So you watched me fuck Laura, little Eve? How naughty you are. Shall I smack your ass to teach you a lesson?" Brenton caught her other nipple and sucked it hard before lifting his head away and staring into her eyes. "Some women like it. A

137

hard hand landing on their ass. Some like to watch a round of fucking too. I think you are one of those rare women, Eve, who enjoys her body but doesn't let her pussy dictate her life."

Brenton's hands cupped the side of her head to stare into her eyes. "I'm going to enjoy being your man."

She jerked slightly because his words rang with so much possession, it almost felt like he was branding her forehead right then with his gaze. His grip tightened as his chocolate eyes burned into hers. "Oh yes, Eve, you've offered me the temptation and I'm going to take it, take you, teach you. Are you a virgin?"

"Of course." Now she was outraged but Evelyn truly could not fault Brenton for asking. She was standing there with her nipples wet from his mouth while her fingers toyed with his cock. Exactly what did she expect the man to think of her?

"There's a part of me that wishes you weren't," Brenton growled through his teeth as he let her head go and found her nipples again. "Shocking?" A harsh laugh came from his chest. "I want to shove up into your pussy so bad it's tearing a hole in my brain."

Brenton stepped back from her and let his eyes scan her from head to foot. His lips pressed together in a tight line as he moved back to her face. In that single moment, Evelyn felt more beautiful than she had ever felt in her entire life. By society's dictates, she was too tall and her hips too broad, her hands weren't delicate but capable and her feet didn't fit into tiny fashionable shoes.

Yet Brenton wanted her. It blazed in his eyes and she actually saw the battle he was waging for control over his inner beast. She had driven him to that edge—her. They understood each other on some deeper level just then. Brenton's nostrils flared as he stroked his own cock with one hand.

"Get on your knees, Eve, you are going to suck my cock before I get to the task of stretching your tight pussy."

Her knees were already bending before she recognized that she was obeying. Well, honestly, she wanted to try it, taste his cock and see if she could make him groan as Laura had done. Brenton's hand cupped the side of her face as she wrapped her fingers around his staff.

"Lick the head first." His orders were so improper. Evelyn was caught between the need to gasp and laugh. To think that other husbands might insist their proper wives obey in just this way made her eyebrows rise up.

Completely wicked!

Evelyn opened her mouth and licked right up the slit on the crown of his cock. The fluid was slightly salty yet not in the least bit unpleasant. She moved her tongue over the top and to the ridge ringing the head. The fingers on her head tightened as she distinctly heard Brenton suck in a deep breath.

Evelyn sent her tongue around that ridge completely before she relaxed her jaw and took the crown between her lips.

"Christ!" His hand on her head shook and it sparked off another rise of boldness from her pride. She might be on her knees but she controlled Brenton.

Opening her mouth wider she took half of his cock deeply into her mouth. His hips jerked and then began pumping against her. He was fucking her mouth with sharp jerks that sent his cock in and out of her mouth. Tightening her fingers around the length of staff still outside her lips, she slid her grip in time with his thrust.

"Every virgin should have to watch a good tumble before her wedding night!" Brenton's thrusts became faster a second before he cussed low and deep. A thick stream of fluid exploded from his cock, flooding her mouth as he thrust hard against her lips. Evelyn swallowed it all as she used her tongue to stroke the ridge circling his cock.

One of Brenton's hands landed on the table with a loud smack as he leaned forward and panted. Evelyn listened to the sound and smiled with triumph. It was amazing how the knowledge that she had brought him to such a state made her feel. Yes, Brenton drove her to the edge of sanity but she could do it in return, too.

Perhaps equality for women wasn't such an outrageous idea after all!

He still wanted to fuck her. Brenton felt the bite of orgasm eat at his cock but the thing still demanded the tight grip of a pussy. Not just a pussy, he craved Evelyn's body. Her hair was still in its prim schoolmarm bun as she sat there licking drops of cum off his cock. Dark ideas of possession filled his thoughts as she raised her head. Moving through his brain was a thick need to bind her to him, mark her with his scent and pump his seed into her belly. She was a treasure that he had discovered and Brenton didn't want to let his prize go.

A smile lifted the corners of his mouth as he caught the scent of her wet pussy. It was going to be his personal pleasure to take her where her prim and proper world never even hinted she could.

Brenton lifted her right off her knees. His strength truly was amazing. Her feet never touched the floor. He sat her on the tabletop and grabbed two handfuls of her skirt too. The cool night air hit her legs as he tucked her skirt up.

"Place your hands on the table behind you and lift your bottom." Evelyn held no understanding of what he was going to do but the burning in her passage was nearing a level that she could not endure any longer. She needed…oh…something. The polished wood was cool as her palms connected with the table behind her. She lifted her bottom as Brenton reached under her skirts. A moment later he dragged her knickers right down her hips and legs. A smile flashed his teeth at her a moment before he tossed the garment over his shoulder.

"Whoever created those damn things should be shot. It was probably some tailor trying to hook more money out of his wealthy clients. Lower-class women don't wear them."

"They don't?" Indeed! No knickers! Her mother was going to haunt her just for knowing that. Brenton hooked one of her legs with his hand and lifted it until he could pull the bow on the top of her shoe.

A few moments later, both her shoes and her stockings were on the floor. Brenton smoothed his hand up her bare leg as he smiled. "You are delectable, did you know that, Eve? Your mother knew what she was doing when she named you after the original temptress."

Brenton sank to his knees and his shoulders spread her thighs wide. She had never felt so vulnerable before and Brenton wanted to increase the distance between her thighs. He pressed on her inner thigh as he moved closer to her spread sex.

"Lean back again, Eve. I think it's time I taught you what your little clit can do in the hands of the right man." His fingers spread the folds of her sex open and she felt his breath hit that spot that had been throbbing for attention. Clit? Another new word, as well as idea. Who might have thought she'd find herself spread wide as a man looked at the most forbidden place on her body.

Brenton leaned forward and licked right up the center of her sex. The action was so shocking her bottom twitched up off the table, but one of his hands clamped over her hip and he spread her folds between his thumb and forefinger.

"It's my turn to suck you."

Evelyn felt her eyes go round in wonder. "Are you going to put your mouth on my...um..."

"Pussy?" Brenton chuckled as he looked up at her startled face. "I plan to lick your slit." His finger slid from the top of her sex to the opening at the back. "Taste your pussy." One of his fingers actually penetrated her passage making pleasure shoot into her belly. It felt so good to have that aching passage filled. "And then, I am going to suck on your clit until you come." His finger left her body and slid up her slit to the little throbbing button at the top of her folds. He pressed the tip of that finger over that one spot and her bottom jerked again. This time she was jerking towards that pressure. Craving more, harder pressing. Indeed, she felt a frantic need to lift her bottom towards Brenton.

Brenton leaned towards her and his tongue lapped her from front to back. Pleasure twisted her as his mouth was almost too hot to tolerate on her tender flesh. But the sensation was so intense she lifted her bottom and offered him her spread body.

His mouth caught that little button at the top of her sex and sucked. Pleasure twisted her tighter than a towel as you wrung it. The tip of his tongue worried it as he sucked. Her thighs wanted to wrap around him and clamp him against her clit. Evelyn listened to the little cries coming from her throat as though they came from a stranger.

Her pussy ached worse than ever as Brenton worried her clit again. She was frantic for release of some kind, her hips jerking up in a rhythm that matched the same one Brenton had used to fuck her mouth.

One thick finger suddenly thrust hard into her pussy and her body snapped like a leather whip. Pleasure so intense it should have had its own word went flooding out from her clit and into her pussy. She actually felt the walls of her sheath trying to grip Brenton's finger and milk it. Her lungs couldn't fill but Evelyn didn't care, she was frozen in that moment of mind-numbing sensation where absolutely everything centered around her clit and pussy.

Brenton pushed to his feet and caught her body with one sturdy arm. Evelyn was sure she would have collapsed to the tabletop if he hadn't. She was also quite certain she didn't have enough of her wits left working to care if her head hit that hard surface.

"Sweet, sweet Eve, if you had any idea how much I enjoyed doing that to you." Evelyn lifted her eyes and gasped. Brenton's words were soft but his eyes betrayed the animal breaking free from inside him. It actually frightened her a bit to see him glaring at her like that...as if she were his intended meal. The head of his cock touched her slit as he held her and her clit began to throb once again. "I think I'll suck you off first every time before I fuck you just to hear you whimper like that."

Deep inside her belly, her pussy contracted with the need to be stretched like his words promised. She wanted to be fuller than she was on his finger... She wanted to be fucked.

Evelyn lifted her bottom and the head of his cock slipped into the fluid coating her opening. The skin protested as she lifted even higher trying to take the head inside her pussy. A hard hand landed on her hip to press her back down and away from his cock. A whimper escaped her lips, shaming her with its plea but she was powerless to hold it back as her pussy sent up a demand so strong everything else fell into nothingness. There was only Brenton and the need burning in his eyes.

"You're too tight, Eve. My cock will tear you."

"But I want it, Brenton. I believe I even need it inside me."

He thrust a finger inside her instead. It eased the hunger for a mere moment before she noticed how much more she wanted. She wasn't full and the craving for more drove her.

Brenton let her go and she caught herself on her hands again. He smoothed his palm over her thighs and pushed them wide. "Stay right there."

He moved across the floor into the dark as Eve felt the cold of the night air. Light came back with him as he brought the candle from the doorway and sat it on a window mount three feet from them. She suddenly felt vulnerable as the light bathed her position. Brenton's eyes moved over her spread pussy and his lips tightened. His cock still jutted out of his open fly as he lifted another item he'd retrieved from across the room.

It was his over-jacket. He reached into the pocket and pulled a fabric bundle from it. He unrolled the thin cotton on the tabletop until an ivory object met her eyes.

Chapter Four

ဆ

"What is that?" Evenly held her voice low as she stared at the object Brenton had unwrapped from the length of cotton. Whatever it was, it looked like a cock. Only it was smaller than Brenton's staff. There was also a polished wooden peg inserted where a cock would join a man's body.

"Do you trust me, Evelyn?" His hand stroked her bare thigh in a soothing motion. Evelyn almost laughed aloud. Trust him? Good Christ! Her knickers were on the floor and her thighs spread wide by his hips. If that was not faith then she knew not what was!

Brenton chuckled at her expression as he smoothed his large hand over her thigh again, this time towards her aching center. His fingertips braised over her wet folds and onto her little clit. Pleasure shot up into her passage as he rubbed the little button. A moment later two thick fingers thrust deep into her body. She heard the little wet sounds of penetration as a moan came from her throat.

Oh yes! She needed to be full!

"Your pussy is too tight for my cock."

Evelyn opened her eyes. A little whimper followed his announcement. She needed more than his fingers inside her. "I'm sorry."

"You are so innocent, Evelyn. All virgins are tight, but my cock is larger than most and I do not enjoy splitting my partners open when there are easier methods of preparing your sweet little body for me." His fingers left her pussy and he wiped her juices on the length of cotton. He reached into the jacket pocket and brought out one more item, this was a jar with a tight seal on the top. There was a little pop as he opened it and sat the lid aside. "This is called a dildo. It's smaller than my cock and I will use it to stretch your pussy." Brenton held the dildo up for her to see clearly. It really was a cock, the top shaped like his cock even down to the detail of the slit and the thick ridge around the crown.

"I've never heard of such a thing."

"Ah, there are so many things I am going to enjoy introducing you to, my dear." His eyes burned into hers as he lowered the dildo. "But only me. I crave you, Evelyn. I shouldn't confess that to you but I do believe I would kill any man I caught sniffing around your body."

Evelyn believed him too. It was written across his face as he watched for her reaction. "There is no one but you for me, Brenton." A dark longing passed over his face as he smoothed her thigh again.

"One stage at a time. There are a hundred delights I want to explore with you, some of them more exotic than others. Tonight, I am going to open your pussy, gently stretching it to hold my cock. Tomorrow I am going to fuck you."

She shivered in response. It was moments like this that Brenton laid out his words like orders. Her pride argued against his assumptions that she would just yield whatever he wished but her flesh quivered as his words filled her mind with dark ideas of forbidden pleasure.

Brenton picked up the dildo again and dipped it into the opened jar. It glistened when he pulled it free. "Brace your hands on the table behind you and lean back. It will hurt but not as much as fucking you would." He brought the dildo towards her spread pussy as she leaned back. The tip of it nudged the folds of her sex apart as Brenton slowly penetrated her with the dildo. Her pussy stretched around the head and then burned as it invaded her deeper.

Brenton's thumb found her clit and rubbed as the burning became pain. He held the dildo still as he pressed on her clit. Her body suddenly relaxed and held the length inside it without pain. There was still a burning but the friction on her clit kept the sensation from becoming true pain.

"That's it. This dildo is three-quarters the size of my cock. Once you take it, I'll be able to ride you without ripping you."

His concern touched her deeply. Somehow, Evelyn doubted that many husbands thought so about their brides on that most talked about wedding night. The few details her friends had dared to share with her spoke of thighs being spread and penetration without any thought to whether or not a bride was wet, much less stretched.

Brenton pulled the dildo free and then thrust it steadily back into her. This time he thrust deeper, opening more of her pussy. His thumb moved on her clit as she was torn between the need to jerk away and lift her bottom towards that penetration.

God, Brenton wanted to fuck her. Rip into her flesh so that she spent every waking hour tomorrow thinking about how hard he'd fucked her. It was a primitive urge that he struggled to keep from taking over his brain. Despite coming in her mouth, his cock was hard enough to shatter as he watched the dildo go where he wanted to be.

Pulling it free, he thrust it smoothly into her pussy. A little wet sound came as it slipped into her pussy. Evelyn actually lifted her bottom as he lodged the last inch of it inside her. She moaned deeply as he began to fuck her slowly. Her pussy got wetter as she lifted her bottom and worked with the motion of fucking. His mouth went dry at the natural way she caught on to the rhythm. His cock begged to join the ride but Brenton gritted his teeth and worked the dildo up into her pussy instead. Trust wasn't given, it was earned. There were far more shocking things he wanted to do to her, with her, and gaining her trust was key.

His cock would have to wait until she was ready for it.

"Fuck me, Brenton! With your cock." Evelyn shouted it exactly like he did. She wanted him to obey her! "The dildo doesn't hurt anymore, I want your cock inside me."

He growled at her demand. His nostrils flared as he thrust the dildo up inside her with a hard thrust. It wasn't enough, her pussy wanted more, she craved his skin against hers as her body was penetrated. Her clit throbbed but she wanted a deeper release than he could give her at a polite distance.

"I am not a delicate porcelain doll, Brenton, I want it all."

He growled again but also pulled the dildo from her. It clattered on the tabletop as his hips pressed her thighs wider. His nostrils still flared as she listened to the harsh rasp of his breath. It was odd to notice that while she was the one spread open for his taking, she, in truth, held control over him. Need made him yield to her demands and it empowered her to lean even farther back as she felt the first touch of his cock against her pussy.

"You belong to me, Evelyn." His cock stretched her body as it thrust forwards. She gasped as his hands clamped around each of her hips to hold her in place. "Say it, tell me your pussy is mine."

Brenton didn't move. He froze with only half of his cock in her and Evelyn moaned for the rest of it. But his eyes blazed into hers as sweat beaded on his forehead. "Tell me."

"You are the only man I have ever allowed to touch me." His cock left and she cried out but she couldn't pledge more of herself to him. He would walk away someday and she would be left with her promise. Men did not have the same understanding of the heart that women did.

"All right, I'll take that…for now." His hands tightened and his hips flexed between her thighs. She was suddenly split open as his cock plunged deep. He held her impaled on that huge cock as she sucked in a gasp of air and her pussy burned. "Easy, Eve, just breathe."

Her body ached but shivered with delight at the same time. Having his cock inside her satisfied a deep yearning she had never noticed was there before. Her blood surged out from her heart as every thought centered around Brenton. The scent of his skin, the bite from her pussy as he opened her for his use.

Oh, it was primitive but there with only a single candle to witness their behavior, Eve didn't care any longer as long as the ache in her belly was fed completely. She felt like she might die if she didn't have that craving from the darkest part of her satisfied.

She lifted her eyelashes and aimed a demand at Brenton. His nostrils flared in response as his hands tightened on her hips. A moment later his cock pulled free and then was thrust deep inside her. His hands held her in place as he leaned against her body and fucked her. Her thighs wrapped around his hips and he growled with approval.

"You were made for fucking, Eve." Hard, wet sounds came from her pussy as he increased his pace. "You might never get another full night's sleep once I toughen up your pussy."

Brenton tried to control his speed but his cock ruled him. Evelyn's pussy contracted around him as she began to climax and it pulled him into the current of pleasure with her. He swore as his seed erupted from his sac and pumped up into her womb. Her pussy milked him as her hips bucked under his hard jerks. She sobbed in his arms as he wrapped his arms around her back to bring her against his chest.

Right then, Brenton found perfection. It was laced with the heavy scent of Evelyn's climax and the musk of his own seed. It sounded like the little whimpers of his woman as she lingered in the glow of deep satisfaction, and he opened his eyes to see that her hair was spilling from its bun, the pins lying on the surface of the table. He plucked the last two from her hair as he smoothed a hand through the dark curtain of silk so that it flowed freely.

Brenton scooped her up in his arms and carried her to her bed. Evelyn was so relaxed she let her head rest against his shoulder. Her ear caught the beat of his heart before he laid her among her bedding. She sighed because he would leave her now. Men and women did not sleep together. The newest science said each heart had its own rhythm and sleeping in the same bed could cause one heart to be disrupted by the other. Mothers were warned against cuddling their babes too much as well.

Brenton sat on the edge of the mattress and the ropes holding the mattress in the box frame creaked. One of his boots hit the floor and then another. He stood up and shucked his fine wool trousers like a fisherman fresh on the dock trying to escape the scent of fish on his clothing.

A moment later he rolled into the bed and slid an arm under her waist to lift her towards him. Evelyn braced her hands on his chest as she landed on her belly facing him.

"Are you mad, Brenton? We cannot sleep together."

His hand pushed the center of her back down and her arms bent at the elbow under his strength. He clasped her in place as her head landed on his shoulder.

"Another stupid dictate from men who think sex needs to be a gentle chore best done quickly and silently." His hand smoothed through her unbound hair as Evelyn tried to find some strength to argue with him. It was the honest truth that she liked being there next to him. A wave of contentment washed over her as her fingers threaded through his chest hair.

"Go to sleep, Eve. This is what it means to have a man." Brenton tipped her chin up to look at her face. "Get used to me."

Her eyes fluttered shut as Brenton frowned. Sleeping with a woman could be comfortable but this was a hell of a lot more. A deep need radiated from his brain to lie in her bed and ensure that her sheets smelled like him. God damn it to hell but he wanted her to always see his face when she lay down at night.

His partners had never been that important before, but Eve was. All he wanted to do right then was raise his knee and part her thighs enough to get his cock back inside her. He should be done with her but getting back inside her pussy was the only thought in his head.

Obsession? Or was it corruption of his soul from the indulgence of lust? Maybe God was finally going to smite him because he'd soiled an innocent this time. Brenton had the feeling that it was going to be far worse than that.

It was just possible he was falling in love.

Chapter Five

ဢ

Brenton kissed her before he left the next morning. Evelyn woke as his warm lips moved over hers in a slow, intimate kiss. His tongue slipped over her bottom lip before thrusting smoothly into her mouth.

Evelyn reached for his shoulders and frowned when she found his shirt covering his skin. She opened her eyes to see him sitting on the edge of the bed as he played with a handful of her hair. The long brown silk was tangled over her bedding and a smug smile sat on his lips as he looked at her disheveled condition.

"I'm going now because I promised you I'd keep our relationship private." His eyes narrowed as he let her hair filter through his fingers. "But I wanted you to know why I left and that I will be back. There's a kettle on the stove just starting to steam. You've got an hour before the breakfast whistle." A hard kiss was pressed to her mouth before Brenton stood up and walked to the doorway. His shoulders disappeared and a moment later she heard the click of the bolt being unlocked.

Evelyn became convinced she was going to hear the sound of that bolt sliding and unsliding for the rest of her days. Her cheeks burned with color as she flung the coverlet aside and sat up. Her eyes rounded with shock as her lower body twisted in pain. It didn't linger but her pussy was sore when she moved.

Setting her teeth firmly together, she stood up. Her bare toes brushed over the wood floor as she caught sight of her bare body in the dressing mirror. Evelyn froze as she considered her reflection. Truthfully, she could not ever remember looking at her body.

She still wore her corset and chemise. The tail of that chemise hung to her mid-thighs and the candle burning on the sink showed her thighs behind the thin silk. Her undergarments were an indulgence that taxed her purse greatly.

But she adored the feel of silk next to her skin. Perhaps that should have forewarned her that she was prone to indulgences of the flesh.

The corners of her mouth twitched up as she pressed the two front halves of her corset towards each other until the first metal busk hook popped open. A busk was essential for a practical woman like herself who didn't have a maid to lace her stays. Once the corset was tightened, you could remove it by working the latches running down the center front open. It took a bit of effort but allowed her to stay in fashion somewhat without the expense of a servant.

Dropping the corset over a chair, Evelyn reached for the tail of her chemise and tugged the garment up and over her head. She aimed her gaze at her reflection as she took the first true look at her bare body in a very long time. Women were taught to avoid looking at themselves, there were even ladies' manuals published that dictated dressing routines that reduced the chances of seeing any bare skin. Those books also told you to bath in a chemise.

Evelyn sighed as she went into the front room to fetch the kettle. The tub was already full of water. Evelyn stared at the water and the plain fact that Brenton must have pumped it into the tub before he woke her. No one, besides her mother, had ever pumped her bathwater for her—a man doing it for his mistress was unheard of. Yet, Brenton had done it for her to ease her body this morning. It was such a tender gesture, two little tears slipped from her eyes. Oh, she was being silly to become so emotional over a bath, but the fact that Brenton didn't have to do it and still did, made her feel cherished by him. Beyond the use of her body, he took time to care about her comfort.

Pouring the hot water into the cold, Evelyn quickly pinned her hair up and stepped into the tub. The water felt delightful against her skin but she did not have time to linger. Ladies might soak in their baths with scented soap but she had students to teach.

The soap provided was common but efficient. Her skin tingled as she scrubbed it and she even smoothed that bar over her thighs and between her legs. Her pussy gave another twitch of pain and her cheeks burned again.

Yet it wasn't shame. Instead it was an odd mixture of surprise and excitement. Never once had she considered that there were parts of her body that could feel such sheer volumes of pleasure. She had never been taught that there were different parts of her genitals much less the names.

The little button at the top of her slit softly throbbed as she touched it with her fingertip. Clit, well, there was a word that quite frankly every woman ought to know, after all, it was sitting right there between her own thighs! Whoever had decided it needed to be ignored had certainly never had it sucked!

If that made her a fallen woman, so be it. She did not regret last night. If Brenton never visited her bed again, she would hold the memory dear. Evelyn stood up and looked at the bed. Brenton would be back. She had seen that promise in his eyes along with a burning hunger that she did not understand. But the memory of his arms around her was the true reason she knew he would return. If sex motivated him, Brenton would have left soon after his cock released its seed. Instead he had cuddled her close and demanded she stay there the entire night. Evelyn didn't know just why.

Yet she craved to know more. Last night Brenton had said he was getting her ready by stretching her with that dildo...yet, ready for what? They had fucked — wasn't that the most forbidden thing?

As she reached for her knickers, a shiver shook her. Excitement began to hum through her as she dressed, because if fucking her was only a beginning, the pleasure awaiting her must be incredible.

That was, if she had the courage to surrender her body to it. Her morals argued against it while her body encouraged her to embark on a journey of discovery with Brenton as her guide.

As she finished dressing and began to pin her hair back into its prim bun, she shivered at the disaster that could befall her. The good mothers out there would not have their children in her schoolroom if they even suspected she had spent last night with her thighs spread on the parlor table. The fact that she had willingly sucked a cock would have her running from a mob. Society was completely unforgiving of weak flesh.

That left Evelyn with a very large dilemma. Live with her cravings or indulgence at the price of her school.

Damn it all!

* * * * *

By midmorning, Brenton was concocting his tenth excuse to leave his work and go see Evelyn. He snorted at his own impatience and flipped open another book of boring figures. His cock refused to lie down and wait. If he couldn't read the calendar himself, he'd question just how old he really was. This manner of constant hard-on was for the boys just growing their first whiskers, not for a man of thirty-four years.

Who would have guessed? Brenton was caught in the most intense reaction he'd ever had to a woman, especially a virgin. He knew there were rare women out there who donned the respectable mantle of lady during the day but gleefully tore it away when night fell. His brother had found one, but him? He was a colored man, and there weren't many white women, even lower-class ones, who would overlook his heritage. Half-white didn't mean anything next to the half-colored part as far as most non-colored folks were concerned.

He'd learned a long time ago to live his life to please himself and stop searching for contentment in other people's opinions. A man had to make his own way if he wanted to find happiness in this world.

Evelyn had never once looked down her nose at him. A large smile covered his face because he just couldn't stop thinking about the pure abandonment she'd gifted him with last night. There was always the possibility she tolerated him for the sake of his position and money but he hadn't promised her anything. Most gold diggers extracted a few pledges before they yielded their bodies. That was always the time he left. He didn't pay for his fucking. He was happy to share passion but he didn't pay his partners and he didn't take bribes from rich women who wanted to control him either. The world out there was an odd mixture of hypocrisy. More than one elegant lady had sent him a card trying to set up a rendezvous because she wanted a colored cock in her cunt for a change.

No, Evelyn didn't want his money. His smile faded as a dark longing took over his thoughts. What she craved was the forbidden pleasures of the flesh. Locked behind her little prim and proper facade was a flame so hot, it just might match his own inner fire.

Pulling a card from his desk, Brenton dipped a pen into his inkwell and composed a short message. The need to press Evelyn was growing by the hour, staying away from her was eating a hole in his brain. He needed to know the depths of her trust and more importantly how hot her longings truly ran.

Sealing the card, Brenton rang a small brass bell that sat on the corner of his desk. The door opened as his accountant stepped into the office.

"My brother should be in the city today, have Clayton take this to him. Leave it with no one else."

"Yes, sir." Clayton was gone a moment later as Brenton stood up and walked through the supply hallway. He caught Evelyn's scent as he heard the first sounds of her voice. He didn't show himself to the rows of students intent on their lesson but he soaked up their bright eyes as they followed Evelyn's explanation and they repeated after her.

She fit into his life rather perfectly on the surface. Now he was going to discover how deep that connection went. His gut twisted as he considered the bet he was about to make. It was double or nothing.

What he craved might send her screaming for justice but it just might seal her in his embrace forever.

As well as his brother's.

He and Nigel shared a common taste for sharing their women. It took their bond to the deepest level and Brenton needed to know if Evelyn could embrace that craving. Not telling her about it would be living a lie and he would rather be lonely than dishonest.

That was a lesson he'd learned from his father. The man had lived a divided life between a lady wife and a mistress. Brenton wasn't willing to walk that path. A man wasn't worth spit if he wasn't honest in his opinion. When he gave his name to a woman, she would know him...completely.

Or he would walk away.

* * * * *

The supper whistle blew and her students jumped from their desks. Their heads nodded to her but their eyes were bright with thoughts of a warm meal. They filed out of the schoolhouse like a well-trained band of recruits, their black leather shoes kicking up the dust in the main compound as they began to frisk and run now that they were clear of the schoolhouse and its rules.

Evelyn turned and went into her parlor to get her cape from where it hung on the wall hook. A metal click hit her ears and she froze. Her nose actually twitched and caught the scent of Brenton's male skin. Honestly, she had never noticed how good a man could smell. Her nipples drew into little hard buttons as she turned to see him watching her from the doorway.

"If you go to the eating hall, I believe I will have to toss you over my shoulder like a desert barbarian and carry you off to my harem." Brenton moved and Evelyn felt a blush burn her cheeks because he was completely bare. Not a stitch of clothing to cover his hard body and her eyes feasted on the sculpted muscles that covered his limbs. But her eyes settled onto his cock and refused to move as she looked at the hard erection pointing right at her.

How strange to consider that blunt physical condition as a compliment. Lust and love were considered two very separate emotions, but right then Evelyn found that one was leading her to the other. Brenton was winning her affections little by little and the fact that his cock was hard in response to her made her heart warm. He could very well have taken that erection off to Laura or ten others like her.

"Would you like to hear my confession, Evelyn?" Brenton moved towards her and took her forgotten cloak from her fingers. He placed it back on the wall hook as he cupped her chin in his large hand. His eyes were alight with desire as he leaned towards her mouth. "I wanted to carry you off like an animal. There's a part of me that craves knowing every man who sees you knows your sweet pussy is milking my cock."

She gasped and his mouth claimed a kiss. It was a hard kiss that demanded entry. Brenton thrust his tongue deeply into her mouth as his words echoed in her head. Her clit pulsed in response to his crude words. She actually felt fluid begin to ease down the inner walls of her pussy as that little pleasure center at the top of her slit pounded with the same rhythm as her heart.

"Does that frighten you, Evelyn?"

Evelyn lifted her eyelids as Brenton broke their kiss and stepped away from her. His question was a test of some sort. His eyes watched her face, waiting to see what manner of response she had. "Truthfully, it excites me." Her words should have shamed her. Instead they unleashed a wave of heat that traveled down her body, awakening every inch of her skin as her body demanded Brenton make good on his words and fuck her until her pussy milked his cock.

Sweet Jesus, she took him to the very edge of sanity. Brenton felt his control stretch as Evelyn eyed his cock. His nostrils flared as he caught the scent of her pussy. There were so many things he needed right at that moment. He needed to fuck, he needed to bare her, but most of all Brenton craved her trust.

Brenton caught her hand in his and walked towards the bedroom. He pulled her with him as she struggled to form a complete sentence. All her brain wanted to do was notice the cut of his bare buttocks. "Brenton, what will your overseers say if we both do not appear at supper?"

"I doubt anyone of them will confess they believe we are fucking the night away, even if one of them suspects it." He sounded disappointed by that idea as he pulled her towards the bed. A single candle burned on the bedside table and there was that little jar of lubricant sitting beside it with the top already open.

A different dildo was lying there, this one was thick and short. A red glow filled the room because Brenton had filled the little stove with a shovel full of coal. The room was quite warm as ruby light crept from the outer room into the darker shadows surrounding the bed.

"My overseers will think you were worked well and hard by your first day and they will fully approve of you collapsing in your bed." Brenton cupped her chin again as his lips turned up into a grin. "I will be happy to make sure that is exactly what you do."

Brenton let her go and it confused her. He lay down on the bed on his side and propped his head onto his hand that was braced by an elbow. His opposite hand firmly gripped his cock and gave the length a stroke. "Do you want me to fuck you?"

Another test question. Brenton stroked his cock as her clit increased its demand. The blunt language intensified the heat burning through her blood. Her mouth actually went dry as she saw the glitter of ruby light shimmer off the first drop of cum as it appeared in the eye of his cock.

"Yes."

"Disrobe for me, Evelyn. Stand right there and take your clothing off, one piece at a time and don't forget to let that silk curtain of hair down as well."

"You want to watch me?" Evelyn was staring at his naked cock and that idea still shocked her. Brenton smiled at her but it wasn't a friendly expression. It spoke of a hunger for her submission as well as her flesh.

"Did you enjoy watching me fuck Laura?"

She had! Brenton chuckled at the expression of wonder that took over her features. He raised a finger at her. "Yes, I want to watch you undress. Watching can be quite stimulating."

Her nipples were in complete agreement. They shrieked for freedom from her stays as the idea of being the center of attention took root in her brain. Yes, she was the one obeying, but Brenton's eyes would be the slaves to her motions.

Yet how did one begin disrobing for an audience? Evelyn looked at Brenton's nude body and felt her confidence rise. She raised her fingers to her collar and began pushing the buttons through their holes. Brenton's eyes followed each one as she worked them down to her waist.

Her dress jacket slipped down her arms and she laid it over a chair back. Her breasts rose over the top of her corset as she reached for the hooks holding her skirt band around her waist. Both the bustled top skirt and the bottom one were stitched into the same band, one little tug and they dropped down her legs, exposing her knickers.

Brenton's mouth pressed into a hard line as Evelyn stepped out of her puddle of skirts and bent to retrieve them. A harsh rasp of his breath made her look up to see his eyes watching the way her breasts jiggled as she bent over. There was no way to miss that he enjoyed the view, and another wave of confidence filled her.

To think that her natural body was quite attractive as it was, without corset and bustle to force the flesh into fashion's model of perfection. Truly, Evelyn had never considered that nature could craft something that would make a man look at her exactly like Brenton was at that moment. She refused to think it was wrong. Never once had she felt so attractive or desired, not in the most expensive dress that she had ever owned.

"I hate those knickers." Brenton stared at her thighs as his fingers moved on his cock again. "Don't wear them."

"Indeed, Brenton, what manner of woman walks out without knickers?"

His eyes shot her a warning. Evelyn had no idea what manner of warning yet her stomach twisted as he placed his feet on the floor and abandoned his lazy sprawl. That simply, the balance of control shifted between them and she felt the impending need to step back from his huge body. A vision of his ability to spring at her and capture her body, filled her mind as her fingers froze on her busk.

"The kind of woman who enjoys knowing her man can back her into a corner and fuck her up against the wall any time he meets her during the day." Brenton stood up and her lungs froze in her chest. He cut through the dark and cupped her face with his hand as he dropped a whisper of a kiss onto her lips.

A mere moment later he bent and slapped his hands on her thighs, and slid them up under the tail of her chemise until he found the waistband of her knickers. He gave a twist and the drawstring snapped. He hefted her off her feet with one arm as his other hand dragged the garment down her legs and off completely.

"I swear I've never enjoyed the scent of a pussy more than I do yours." Brenton felt his muscles shake as he caught a full breath of her aroused body. The beast inside him was attracted to that scent like a stallion was to a mare's heat. Nothing mattered but mounting her and getting his cock inside her wet pussy.

Evelyn gasped as her back hit the wall. Brenton lifted her and his hips spread her thighs as she grasped his shoulders with her hands. The head of his cock nudged the folds of her slit open as he kept moving towards her until their bodies were flush and his cock began to penetrate her. His hands held her bottom as his hips flexed and then he thrust deep into her body as she listened to her own moan. Pleasure spiked through her as her clit cried with the demand for friction. Brenton moved between her thighs, and his cock left and then thrust hard back into her.

"Oh yes..." The words were just an extension of her body's demands. There was no thought, only need. Brenton snarled softly against her neck as his teeth bared and bit the tender skin. The little pain zipped down her spine and joined the pleasure ripping into her belly. At that moment she wanted him to take her, she needed the hard possession that proved he was stronger than her. His hips flexed and his cock slammed back into her pussy. His fingers tightened around the cheeks of her bottom, holding her as his cock rammed in and out of her spread body. Evelyn sobbed as her clit pounded and Brenton fucked her even harder. His teeth bit her once more as climax ripped her away from the world and spun her into a vortex of spinning pleasure. Brenton snarled next to her ear as he thrust deeply and she felt the hot spurt of his seed hit her womb. Her thighs clamped around his hips to hold him in place as the walls of her pussy gripped and pulled his cock.

Chapter Six

ɞɔ

"Leave your damn knickers off." Brenton still growled the words but Evelyn smiled at the need edging his voice. She did that to him. His shoulders shook slightly as she smoothed her fingers over the tense muscles. Her stomach growled and his head lifted from her neck. His lips curled back to show her a smug smile.

"Finish undressing and we'll eat."

Brenton let her down and walked back into the parlor. Evelyn began to work the metal fastenings on her busk as she giggled. She just could not hold back her amusement as she considered they were going to dine—naked. Reaching for a shoe, Evelyn unlatched it and sat it aside. She did the same to the other foot, before rolling each stocking down her leg. This was certainly going to be an odd way to share a meal with a gentleman.

Well, with a man. Here there were no genteel codes of conduct to observe. In their place were the rules of nature, and Evelyn found them quite satisfying. Her corset came free and she laid it aside. She hesitated as she fingered the tail of her chemise. Brenton was watching her, she could feel his eyes on her and she shivered as she pulled that last barrier up and over her head. The fear that he might not like what he found beneath her stays sent a shudder down her body. Women were always tightening their laces to compress the waistline because tiny was the fashion. Her natural waist was certainly not sixteen inches.

"You're a very beautiful woman, Evelyn." Brenton's voice was deep and husky as he stood in the doorframe and stared at her. His gaze moved down her body slowly taking note of each curve. In a way, it was rather odd to feel so vulnerable because he was just as naked as she. Maybe it was not the fact that they were bare that truly bothered her, perhaps it was concern over Brenton's desire to stay with her now that she had let him fuck her.

Their eyes met and his were full of enjoyment. It was a deep emotion that looked like it went beyond the pleasure of the flesh. His lips rose into a grin as he balanced a tray on one hand.

Her nose caught the scent of food as he came closer. Brenton passed right by her and rolled his frame onto her bed once more. He patted the surface of the mattress with a single hand as he took the cotton towel off the top of their dinner. He broke a round of bread in two and offered one side to her.

"Come here, Eve."

Evelyn did but she nibbled on her lower lip as she went. "Why do you sound like you are going to test me, Brenton?"

His face tightened almost ominously. Evelyn stared at the guarded expression as she stretched out the same as he was with only the tray of food between them. Brenton lifted one hand and stroked her cheek as his eyes considered her while his jaw worked on a mouthful of bread.

"Fucking you isn't the most scandalous thing I'd like to do with you."

Now that did shock her, yet not in a bad manner. Excitement flared up as her imagination tried to conceive of anything that might be more forbidden than what they had already done. Her brain failed her, though, try as she might she truly could not fathom what surpassed what they had already done.

But she shivered as more excitement rose at the idea of the unknown and the fact that Brenton wanted to take her deeper into those shadows.

"Then what is?"

She really wanted to know. Brenton stared at her bright eyes and fought the urge to play it safe. Hellfire and damnation, he didn't want to lose what he had. For the first time in his life he understood why his father might have chosen a wife who didn't share his passion of the flesh. The heart had more influence than he'd ever suspected it could, especially on him.

But that didn't change the needs burning away at his brain. Dark images of Evelyn pressed between him and his brother that would haunt him forever if he hid them. Right, wrong, it was part of him, a piece of that inner beast that every man had caged inside his self-control.

"Sharing you with another man." Brenton's eyes lit with his statement. Evelyn felt her brain freeze around that single idea. Two men and her?

"That's not possible."

Brenton chuckled at her comment. She amazed him. Right then her forehead was creased as she tilted her head to one side and tried to figure out how one woman could be with two men at once.

"It is if your bottom has been stretched."

Evelyn turned her head to look at the table and the new dildo Brenton had brought tonight. Was it really for her bottom? Not even in the darkest corners had she once heard of something like that.

But the idea of two men tore at her affections for Brenton. What did that mean? Was she a toy to be played with at his whim? His fingers suddenly cupped her chin and brought her eyes level with his.

"I grew up as a child with no place in either the black or white world, Evelyn. My brother was my friend, companion and partner in mischief. But I was his escape as well. Nigel was the only child in a house straining under responsibilities and expectations of the heir. We used to sneak away together as boys and it never stopped even when we grew into men. We shared everything together—we still do."

There was a wealth of meaning in those last three words. Perhaps it wasn't the correct manner of expected behavior but she recognized just how Spencer Industries had grown into the giant it currently was. The men running it were completely devoted to the family name and to each other. Along the lines of rich families, it was simple enough to understand, but could that bond truly reach to the intimate?

Evelyn looked back at Brenton's dildo. Two men at once... The idea tempted her more than she dared acknowledge. Whoever could have imagined that the mind was so full of lust-driven enjoyment? She was losing the ability to see the border between affection and craving. Everything she had ever been taught said she should be able to clearly see that lust had no place among the pristine emotions of the heart. Yet it was all flowing together in a thick stream of sensation and excitement. She didn't want either emotion alone but craved more of the swirling mixture that included every last dark and light delight for her senses.

Brenton cupped her chin again and brought her around to face him. Evelyn stared at the taut features drawn tight by stress. He actually feared her reaction to his words. To see a vulnerability flicker through his eyes made her heart fill. It was not a look any man might fake, it was staring at her as Brenton laid his honest personality out for her to view. That took more courage than she had ever witnessed.

"I fuck you first and last, Evelyn, because you are mine. You will not take another lover unless I am there to share you with him." A hard note of possession rang in his voice.

"And what about you, Brenton? Do you hold yourself to the same restrictions?" It was a bold question, yet Evelyn did not care. In a world controlled by men, it was important to understand the rules and often that meant men expected to have far less restrictions than their female companions. A man might have a wife and take a mistress, but a wife who indulged in a lover was labeled a slut. The mistress was politely overlooked and ignored by everyone.

Well, Evelyn decided that she would not be overlooking any lover. Either she was Brenton's mistress, or she would sleep in her lonely bed without him.

Brenton curled his teeth back to smile at her. He pushed his body up from the mattress and lifted the tray off the bedding. There was a small thud as he sat it on the bedside table and then he grasped her wrist and pulled her towards the top of the bed. Brenton pushed her down until she was lying on her back and he was looming over her. One hand cupped her right breast and pleasure shot down her spine in response. It amazed her to discover that her breasts could transmit so much sensation. The nipple was drawn tight as Brenton gently squeezed and rubbed the mound. "If you will marry me, I will always share my other lovers with you."

Evelyn laughed. She could not stop the sound from shaking her chest. "Brenton, you are wicked to tease me like that! As if you would wed an employee."

"Now I really want to drag you off to church, Evelyn. Do you have any idea how fast Laura would have jumped at the chance to hook me into wedlock? Do you have any idea how fast any other woman would have slapped me for telling them I wanted to share them with my brother?"

It was true enough but Evelyn heard only the ring of honesty in Brenton's voice, how many wives lamented the lack of truth in their husbands? For that matter, how many women lay on their backs and refused to admit that they enjoyed their duties? Life was showing her a side of it that she had never even guessed might be possible. Maybe this was what it meant to be lovers. Frank words that translated into intense pleasure. "Have you shared your sister-in-law?"

"Yes." Brenton stroked one of her cheeks as hunger flickered in his eyes. "She will welcome you to our gatherings. Lynette is a rare gem, like you. She embraces her passion, no matter where it takes her body."

It was more... Evelyn knew in her heart that there was more to the invitation than just her body. If not, Laura would have serviced Brenton's needs well enough. She reached for Brenton's cock and closed her fingers around it. His eyes narrowed with pleasure as the hand on her breast tightened.

"Turn over." Brenton's hand left her breast and his eyes opened wide to blaze at her. Determination flickered in those dark orbs as well as a deep hunger. "Pull your knees up under your belly and spread your thighs."

Brenton didn't wait for her to comply, his hands caught her hips and rolled her over. A tiny curl of fear caught her as her face settled on the sheet and her bottom rose up. She was completely at his mercy and Brenton boldly stroked each cheek of her bottom before he pulled them apart to look at her back entrance.

"I'm going to stretch you, Evelyn, and you will meet me in the country this weekend for a small gathering that will astound you. I'm going to fuck your tight pussy while my brother's cock fills your bottom."

"Will I?" Evelyn actually hated the little tremor of excitement edging her voice. The telltale sound was little better than a white flag of surrender.

Brenton chuckled and smoothed a hand over her bottom. "It's more intense than you can know, Evelyn. The feeling of a cock in your bottom while another one fucks your pussy. You'll scream for more, beg us to use you together." Brenton stroked a finger through her wet slit and circled the opening to her pussy.

Evelyn should have protested. But her pussy gave a shout of need that would have made a liar out of any words spoken in denial. It was simple to trust Brenton because everything he had taught her had far surpassed even her fantasies.

Yet it was more than that. The boldness that sometimes rang in his orders made her shiver. There was a part of her that enjoyed being bent to his commands.

The bed shook as Brenton stood next to it. Evelyn watched his finger dip into the jar and then lift. The ruby light glittered off the lubricant as he carried it to her bottom. She felt the smooth glide of it between her cheeks before Brenton dipped the finger into the jar once more and then spread more of the cool gel on her.

The first penetration made her tense at the unfamiliar sensation. Brenton made a soothing sound above her as one hand held her hip and the other pressed into her bottom. Her heart beat frantically as that finger pressed into her body and then left. Brenton returned to the jar of lubricant and then carried more of it to her bottom.

This time her body relaxed and took his finger. Having her bottom filled pressed the walls of her pussy against themselves. Her clit suddenly pounded with the same rate as her heart as Brenton began to move his finger in and out of her bottom.

"Sweet Evelyn, do you have any idea what a precious gem you are?" His voice was dark and husky as his finger fucked her bottom. He inserted a second one and gently worked it until her body accepted it without protest. Her clit pulsed as her pussy demanded to be filled. A satisfied grunt came from Brenton as he withdrew his fingers.

"Just relax." He picked up the plug from the table and dipped it into the jar. A moment later the tip of the thing was pressed against her bottom. The skin burned as he pressed it forward. Sweat beaded on her skin as it was thrust up into her bottom. Pain tightened her nerves but it did not become agony. Brenton stopped with only part of the dildo inside her and then pulled it free.

He dipped it once again and then pressed it into her body. This time it slid deep, until only the handle was left outside her. The plug filled her, making her frantic for a cock inside her pussy. Her hips gave a jerk as she actually raised her bottom to offer her pussy for that fucking. Evelyn did not think about it, it was an urge that rose from her body just like the need to breathe.

Brenton smacked her bottom instead. Evelyn cried out as his hand landed on one side of her bottom. The little smarting pain zipped straight into her clit, unleashing an insane desire to be fucked. At that moment she would have begged for it. Brenton smacked the opposite side of her bottom instead. Evelyn whimpered and heard a deep chuckle from behind her.

"Like that?" His hand delivered another smack and then two more. "I'll be happy to spank your bottom while you ride my brother's cock." Two more blows landed before Brenton lifted her body and laid her on her back on the bed. His face was harsh as he pushed her thighs apart with almost a violent motion.

"But right now, I need to fuck you. Hard and deep."

Another whimper escaped her mouth as Brenton's body pressed down on top of hers. Brenton caught her hands and pulled them above her head as his hips held her thighs wide. The head of his cock pressed into her slit as he thrust slowly into her. His body shook with the effort of controlling that first thrust. She was almost too full with the plug in her bottom, but he used small, hard thrusts to work his cock into her pussy.

Brenton actually snarled as his cock sank completely into her body. The hair on his chest rasped against her tight nipples as he bent his head and scraped his teeth against the skin of her neck. Her body was so full and it thrilled her. Pleasure shook her as Brenton bit her neck but still didn't move his cock. Evelyn suddenly understood how a deer felt in those final moments before it was killed by a lion. She was completely at Brenton's mercy, his hard, male body holding her for his feasting pleasure. Her bottom still stung from his spanking and that was mixing with the plug stretching her bottom. Her clit was frantic for friction. Her hips tried to lift Brenton's weight and work against his cock. Brenton raised his mouth from her neck and his eyes glittered right above hers.

"Promise me you'll come with me this weekend." His voice was hard as he used his body to hold her in place. The skin was drawn tight over his jaw as he clenched his teeth against the need to fuck her. "I've never invited a woman to meet my brother, Evelyn. Only you."

A tiny whimper escaped her lips as she watched his eyes brighten with need so deep, Evelyn wasn't certain either of them were sane anymore. They had fallen into the deepest pits of each other's souls and stood completely exposed with all of their imperfections on display for each other.

"I will join you."

His hips bucked and his cock slammed hard into her pussy. Evelyn cried out at the sharp pleasure as Brenton's body began to plunge his cock between her spread thighs. Her bottom lifted for his thrusts as she heard his snarl of possession join her whimpers.

Nothing mattered but fucking her. Brenton had never needed to fuck so damn bad in his life before. If he knew for certain his heart would burst from the exertion, that still would not have been enough to make him slow his pace. He pressed her arms to the bed above her head and felt her hard nipples scrape against his chest. Her pussy made wet sounds as he drove his cock hard against her clit. He wasn't deep enough, and his hips drove his cock harder.

"Feel how full you are, Eve?" His cock pulled out and slammed back into her pussy. "Two cocks will be better than one. I want my brother to hear you moan, I want you to hear Lynette scream as I fuck her and you watch my cock split her body. But more importantly, I want the right to fuck you every night. I want everyone to know this pussy is for my cock. I want to lie down next to you and not have to sneak away before sunrise. So marry me."

Evelyn sobbed beneath him as her body jerked and pulsed with climax but he still hadn't fucked her enough. Brenton growled as he refused to let his seed escape with a climax to match hers. The bed ropes groaned beneath the mattress as his hips fucked her harder. The plug in her bottom made her pussy as tight as a fist, but she tightened even more as a second climax ripped through her body. Her head was filled with the image of being pressed between two men. She wanted it so much right then.

Brenton suddenly pulled his cock free and rolled her body over. Evelyn was far beyond caring what he did, as long as he did it to her. With a hand on each hip he pulled her bottom up and spread her knees under her. He pulled the plug from her bottom and then more of the lubricant was smeared over her. The head of his cock pressed against the newly opened entrance as he grasped her hips in hard hands. Evelyn clawed at the bedding as he thrust forward, stretching her more.

"You will marry me, Evelyn, if I have to fuck you in the dining hall to shame you into it!"

Brenton growled his words as his hips thrust his cock deeper into her bottom with small, jerking thrusts. It hurt but mixed with the pleasure radiating from her clit, and Evelyn cried with the motions of that cock because her body needed even more from his. Her pleasure wasn't enough. She wanted to feel the splash of his seed against her flesh, know without doubt that she satisfied his hunger.

Evelyn lifted her bottom for his cock and Brenton felt the last of his control shred. His cock sank into her bottom and there was no holding back the eruption from his sac. His hips jerked as he fucked her bottom and pumped his seed into her. Every muscle he owned shook as his cock finally stopped demanding he fuck.

Brenton pulled his spent flesh from her bottom and rolled Evelyn over. She lay back on the bedding as her lungs worked to draw deep breaths into her body. The scent of her pussy filled his nose as Brenton pressed her thighs wide and spread her slit with his fingers.

Evelyn moaned as his tongue found her clit. It was a low sound of pure rapture. Brenton sucked on her clit and her pussy twisted again. His tongue flickered over the little nub and climax tore her deeply once again. This time her brain floated away on the waves of sensation as she heard Brenton cussing softly above her body.

"We have to bathe, Eve, then I'll let you sleep."

The water in the tub was cold but her skin was still hot so Evelyn sighed as Brenton lowered her into the bath. His large hands began to smooth a bar of soap over her bare breasts and she just couldn't muster the will to protest. Brenton made an efficient maid as he soaped every inch of her skin and then poured more water over her. He lifted her from the tub and wrapped a towel around her before he yanked the plug at the bottom of the tub to release the water.

Brenton turned and cupped her face with both hands. His lips moved across hers as he kissed her long and slow. The toweling fell to the floor as her hands reached for his shoulders. A moment later, Brenton scooped her up and laid her back in her bed. He flipped the bedding over her before flashing her a smug grin and turning back to the tub.

Evelyn turned to see him working the pump to fill the tub once again. It amazed her to find enjoyment in simply watching him go about the common chore of bathing. There was an intimacy in the room that truthfully, she had never felt between herself and another soul on the planet. If Brenton had left the room right then, she was almost certain he would have ripped a piece of her heart away as he left.

The coals had burned down now, leaving the bed in a deep shadow. Brenton came to her and pulled her body next to his as he settled his wide shoulders against the mattress. The warm scent of his skin filled her senses and it was for that moment…absolutely perfect.

Appearances be damned!

Chapter Seven

ဆ

Evelyn woke to an empty bed. She rubbed at her burning eyes and forced her protesting body from the bed. It was actually Friday. Her first week was to be a short one but with her after-hours activities, she was grateful.

A small note was sitting on top of her corset as she reached for it. Her chemise fluttered in the early morning breeze as she broke the seal.

"Tonight a carriage will be waiting for you at the front gate. Leave your knickers off if you want to finish your lessons."

Lessons indeed! Improper ones to be certain. Yet her lips curled up into a smile as Evelyn picked her knickers up and folded them instead of stepping into them.

Her thighs felt odd as she walked through the parlor and unlatched the door to the schoolroom. She caught her reflection and giggled. No one would ever guess that the prim-looking schoolmarm was knickerless.

So improper, yet so completely exciting!

* * * * *

A closed carriage awaited her just as Brenton's note had promised. Evelyn stared at it as excitement built inside her. Looking at her, no one would even suspect that she stood there without knickers on or that she was embarking on a weekend with her lover.

Did anyone even think thoughts such as these? Indeed it would appear that there were those who did but they masqueraded themselves amid the staunch and proper people they lived among.

Brenton was nowhere to be seen. His promise to consider her good name evident as she opened the door and climbed into the carriage. The driver would spill any sighting of the two of them together without chaperone at the first shot of whisky the man downed once he was finished with his duty.

That left her with a long and lonely ride to the Spencer estates. The carriage jerked forward and her heart with it. Evelyn was caught between the excitement and shame of the moment. Two men and one woman, the idea fired her blood. A dark craving to indulge in deeper longings filled her as she surrendered any last hope of denying she needed to know what two men fucking her felt like. Her bottom ached just a bit from Brenton's use but it was far overshadowed by the pleasure that had ripped through her when he fucked her with that plug still inside her bottom.

She was avoiding thinking about his marriage proposal. Indeed, she would be a fool to believe he meant it. Brenton had money and name, even if it was tainted with his darker blood. There were far better brides out there who would bring him money and prestige. She was a schoolmarm and would bring only herself to a marriage. Evelyn was not a simpleton and understood that the world simply did not work any other way. What a man said in passion often did not translate well into the cold realities of the world.

She would have to forgive him that and be content as his lover. Her blood began to race as she thought about the new level of consort the weekend promised to make her into. If Brenton did indeed share everything with Nigel Spencer, that meant the two men had shared Nigel's lady wife.

Evelyn giggled as she considered that indeed, some families were closer than others, apparently.

* * * * *

The Spencer estate was quite a sight to behold as it came into view. Huge whitewashed columns with large windows. The carriage pulled right up to the main steps as the team pulled to a halt.

Evelyn gasped because she was certainly not accustomed to being received at the main entrance of an estate like this one. The schoolmarm might be a high position in the house, but it was still expected that she enter from the back door.

The carriage door was opened by a footman as he offered his gloved hand for her descent to the ground. Her single satchel was already grasped in the hand of an under-footman who inclined his head at her as she shook out her skirts.

"Hello, Evelyn!" A petite lady raised her voice ever so slightly as she came down the white steps. Her body was a study in grace as she held out her gloved hands towards Evelyn.

"Please forgive me for using your Christian name but I confess I am a riot of excitement." She grasped Evelyn's own glove-covered hands and leaned forward to leave a kiss on her cheek. When she was standing in front of Evelyn once more, her eyes sparkled in the lamplight.

"You shall call me Lynette and no curtsies! I am simply beside myself with delight that you shall become my sister! I feared that Brenton would never meet that special lady."

The carriage man choked and tried to stifle the sound as a dry cough. Evelyn felt her eyes round with shock as Lynette shifted her gaze to the driver and then back to Evelyn's shocked expression. She pressed her lips together and fluttered her eyelashes.

"Come inside, my dear, there is so much for us to talk about. You really must confess how you find enough patience to tolerate Brenton's stubborn streak."

Evelyn found her lips pressing tight to contain her own smile at Lynette's cleverly disguised comment. No matter what the present staff might think, there was nothing improper about the lady's words. It would appear that Lynette was indeed a great deal like Brenton. The lady practiced that most intriguing art of keeping up her appearances while meaning so very much more.

The house itself was magnificent. Evelyn was swept along with Lynette as her satchel was handed off to an upstairs headmaid and her hostess took her into the formal parlor.

"I was about to come hunting for you." The man leaning against the fireplace must be Nigel Spencer. He aimed a hard look at Lynette that the lady flung aside with a flutter of her delicate eyelashes. A deep chuckle came from across the elegant room and Evelyn felt her heart accelerate as her ears instantly recognized Brenton.

"Nigel, you are helpless in the hands of your wife."

Nigel covered his heart with one hand and bowed deeply to his brother. "May you suffer the same fate."

Brenton chuckled and moved across the thick Oriental carpet to capture one of Evelyn's hands. His fingers were a stark contrast to the formality surrounding them all but Evelyn secretly enjoyed the fact that he did not don gloves. His pride shone through with that single refusal to bend to society's rules. He was dressed as finely as any gentleman on his way to meet the president, yet his bare fingers declared him his own man who was not going to hide his color for anyone. You would accept him for who he was or this man would not call you friend.

Evelyn looked into his eyes as he placed a kiss on her gloved hand, and felt her heart fill with love. Oh, she could not hide it. It should have been impossible to discover such deep affection for a man that she had not known a week past, yet it was there. Her very presence in the Spencer home was testimony to her trust of him.

Love and trust were twins that rarely left the other behind when they took up residence in a heart. She trusted Brenton for many reasons but she loved him for everything that he was unafraid to display to the rest of the world.

"I would be delighted to suffer the same fate, but you will have to help me convince Evelyn to marry me. She believes my heartfelt declaration was false."

"It would be my pleasure." Nigel Spencer looked like a gentleman but his words were edged with something much darker. Even Lynette's eyes flickered with more heat than a lady was expected to display. Oh, it was all done so subtly, in truth, Evelyn wondered if it was her imagination seeing what she wanted to find.

Yet there was no mistaking the fluid that touched the top of her bare thighs. It was hidden by her skirts but she could not deny the very blunt response her body offered up to Brenton. Either the world was mad or her body was. The inner woman did not agree with the picture the world viewed.

And Evelyn was positive that the other three people in the room felt exactly the same way.

Lynette suddenly rose from a brocade-covered sofa. "Evelyn must be tired after her journey. I bid you good night, gentlemen."

The maid immediately opened the parlor door for her mistress as Lynette took Evelyn by the hand and pulled her along with her. The ladies' bustles moved with their graceful steps as they left the two gentlemen behind. They went up the grand staircase at a slow pace due to their tight corsets but it was more than that. The eyes of the household staff were everywhere. Lynette was making quite certain they were seen together as they left Brenton and Nigel below. There would be no rumor that Brenton had joined her in her bed.

Evelyn dismissed the maid who arrived to help her disrobe. She had never had a dressing maid and truthfully she was uncomfortable giving the woman direction.

The guestroom was larger than her entire living space at the school. Evelyn admired the wallpaper as she shook out her clothing and pulled her nightdress from the closet. There was a bath waiting for her that she eagerly stepped into. A kettle of steaming water had arrived with the maid and Evelyn tipped it into the tub with a little hum on her lips.

With all the new sensations she had recently discovered, she had also noticed that clean skin felt wonderful. It was not that she had let her body become ripe. She just appreciated lying down with freshly scrubbed skin.

The cotton nightgown floated over her skin as she found her brush and sat down to stroke the length of her hair. Darkness invaded the room and took the walls and corners hostage. A single candle burned next to the mirror, casting its glow over her long hair. What a relief it was to sit there in nothing but a nightgown! No corset or tight jacket. No padding on her bottom to make it conform to fashion's rules. She was just relaxed and even her hair lay in long strands, free from her steel hairpins.

The curtains next to the balcony moved as a hidden door silently opened. Evelyn stared at Lynette because the polished lady exterior that had greeted her was completely gone now. Lynette was wearing only a thin silk chemise that the candlelight turned transparent. The garment only fell to her mid-thighs and a pair of very expensive black lace stockings was held up with purple ribbon garters around each of her thighs.

It was shocking to say the least but it also released a flood of excitement that surged through Evelyn. Lynette raised a single eyebrow at her as she offered Evelyn a folded pair of stockings. Evelyn shook her head. She could not be responsible for the care of such a costly pair of stockings! She could smell the scent of silk and knew the stockings must cost half a week's pay.

"Nonsense. Put them on, Brenton will adore you in them," Lynette whispered as she placed them on the table right in front of Evelyn. The lady plucked the forgotten hairbrush from her frozen fingers and laid it on the polished wood surface. She turned and moved towards the bed that the maid had turned the covers down for Evelyn. Lynette yanked two of the pillows from the head of it and stuffed them under the bedding. She tugged on the sheets and coverlet until she had tucked those pillows into the bed to look just like a person.

Evelyn stroked the stockings with a single fingertip, smiling at the smooth silk thread they were made of. So decadent and forbidden, if she wore them, she was accepting gifts for her favors. Her lips turned down into a frown. If that was so, then what exactly were flowers given to a lady by a gentleman appearing at her door to escort her on a turn about the park? Hothouse flowers cost money too.

Picking one up, Evelyn lifted her foot and slid the black lace up over her foot. Her ivory skin showed through the pattern of the lace in an amazing contrast of dark and light. The top of the stocking was crowned with emerald green ribbon. Evelyn reached for the second stocking and caught Lynette's reflection in the dressing table mirror. The lady sent her a naughty grin before Lynette held a single finger to her lips as she used her opposite hand to wave Evelyn forward towards the still open door.

Lynette pinched the candle flame out before she pulled the door shut behind them.

"There! That will keep the maids silent if one of them decides to check on you. They shouldn't but we must do our best to conceal our meetings."

Lynette's voice was edged with the same excitement racing through Evelyn's blood. Although newly acquainted, there was an unmistakable bond between them. Some things you learned just by observation. Lynette's appearance in her chemise and stockings spoke volumes about her views on just what was acceptable when the door was locked for the night.

Her new friend led her down a narrow hallway that, although dark, wasn't pitch-black. There was the yellow glow of light beckoning to them from whatever lay on the other end.

It was another door that stood open to a chamber that was lit by only a very few candles. But what lay inside that room amazed Evelyn.

Both Nigel and Brenton were there. Neither had a stitch of clothing covering their frames. The candlelight bathed their male forms, making Evelyn's mouth water. She could not stop the urge to lower her eyes and look at Nigel's cock. The staff stood away from his body as he watched them enter the room.

Brenton watched only her, though. His eyes were glued to her face as Lynette pulled her into the chamber and firmly shut the door. A little metal click made Evelyn smile.

She was among friends. No, that was too light a term for the inhabitants of the chamber. She was in the company of compatriots. It felt like she had finally managed to make her way home.

Brenton's lips curled back to flash her a wide smile. Relief crossed his face as he moved towards her. Evelyn smiled right back at him, unable to suppress the emotion. There was no reason to, not here. It was a sanctuary where the rules were a polar opposite from the world on the other side of the locked doors.

Here, emotion was the dictator and Evelyn was going to enjoy serving it with every bit of will she had.

"Say you are going to marry me." Brenton's voice told her he expected her compliance. Boldness swelled inside her and lifted her daring to toy with him.

"No." Evelyn used her best schoolmarm voice for that single word. Nigel's bark of laughter came from across the room. Brenton frowned at her before he reached forward and grasped the front of her nightgown. He rent the garment in half with one twist of his huge hands. Evelyn jumped back as the fabric split with a loud sound and she stared in shock as her nightgown stayed in Brenton's hands while she stood in nothing but the lace stockings.

Brenton tossed the ruined gown aside and raised a hand to her. He curled one single finger at her. "Come here, Evelyn."

Evelyn wanted to obey him. How odd the way it felt to be the one submitting. It was more empowering than standing in front of a room full of children who feared her wrath. She stepped forward as Brenton's eyes dropped to her nipples. They were drawn tight as Evelyn heard the sound of Nigel and Lynette kissing across the room. She was torn between the urge to look at Brenton as he watched her and the temptation to look at the other couple.

Her eyes did stray over Brenton's shoulders to see that Lynette was in her husband's embrace. Nigel held her head in one hand as he tipped her head back for a hungry kiss. His other hand was roaming over her bottom as she reached up into his hair.

Brenton caught her around her waist and pulled her against his body. Only he stepped behind her so that she was facing his brother. Brenton's arm clamped around her waist while the hand captured one breast and gently squeezed it. His breath hit her ear as he laid a small kiss onto her neck.

"It's amazing to discover how much watching a couple fuck can arouse you, isn't it, Eve?" He bit her neck and then licked the tiny pain. His fingers pinched her nipple and that pain joined the bite for a moment before it transformed into acute pleasure that flowed down to her clit. "I'm going to enjoy watching you with my brother."

"But…"

Brenton smacked her bottom. Evelyn yelped at the unexpected blow. The right side of her fanny throbbed and that intensified the pulse in her clit. "You will suck my cock and then his, and then, Eve, we are both going to fuck you at the same time. Think about it, my cock in your pussy while my brother's cock tunnels into your bottom." Brenton smacked her bottom again and then twice more as he bent her over his arm. Lynette turned away from her husband's kiss to watch as

Brenton spanked her. Fascination flared in the other woman's eyes as Brenton's hand landed on her bottom several more times.

"Suck my cock, Eve." His command made her shiver as Eve dropped to her knees in front of him. She reached for his erection and closed her fingers around the hard staff. Brenton sucked in a harsh breath as she pulled her clasped hand up his cock and then pressed her hand back to the base of his weapon. Leaning forward she licked the slit on the head and caught the first taste of cum. That excited her even more. Her pussy ached as Evelyn licked the head of Brenton's cock and then took the plum-shaped organ into her mouth. She flicked her tongue on the little spot right under the ridge that always made Brenton tremble. His hand caught her hair and twisted the strands in a tight grip, delighting her. There was something ultra-intense about driving him insane. Evelyn took more of his cock into her mouth as she listened for another sigh that he was straining to hold on to his control. The slit on top of his cock head offered up another few drops of salty cum as she began to move her head up and down on his cock, mimicking a fucking motion as she took his cock deeper into her mouth and then placed her lips tightly around the staff before pulling her head away. The fingers in her hair tightened as Evelyn reached for his seed sac and gripped. Brenton growled as his first offering of seed hit her tongue. She sucked on his cock to draw it from the organ faster and she heard him cuss as she fought to keep her lips tight around his staff and not smile with triumph.

When Evelyn let Brenton's cock go, she looked up to find his lips resting in a satisfied grin. That pleased her because she had placed that expression on his face. She gave his seed sac a last squeeze before she stood up and felt his hand rub one side of her bottom. While satisfaction was still evident on his face there was a deeper need burning in his eyes.

"Now go and suck Nigel's cock." One more hard blow landed on her bottom as Brenton released her. She turned her head to look at him in wonder. Did the man truly mean it? "Go kneel in front of my brother and wrap your lips around his cock, Eve. I'm going to watch you do it. Remember how much you enjoyed watching me fuck Laura? Seeing you work on my brother's cock will make me insane to get inside your pussy."

Just hearing it out loud made her pussy contract. The tops of her thighs were slick as Evelyn moved across the floor. Lynette stepped aside as Nigel cupped one breast and brushed Evelyn's nipple with his thumb. Evelyn looked at Lynette to find her watching with a hungry look that made excitement curl in her belly again.

Evelyn knelt in front of Nigel and cupped the sac hanging below his cock with one hand. He sucked in his breath as she rolled the sac between her fingers and then leaned forward to lick the slit on the head of his cock. There was another swift intake of breath as she closed her mouth around his cock. Evelyn closed her eyes and sucked. One of Nigel's hands gripped her head as his hips gave a jerk and then another. She relaxed her mouth as she allowed more of his cock inside. She could feel Brenton's gaze on her. It made her almost frantic to take more of Nigel's cock into her mouth. The idea that Brenton was watching her suck a cock made her even more frantic to have a cock inside her as she sucked.

Nigel suddenly pulled her head back as he growled down at her. "Enough! I'm going to save my seed for a pussy tonight."

The fact that he didn't name just whose body he was going to climax inside of made it even more exciting. A manner of test, to see which woman drove him over the edge.

A wet sound hit her ears and Evelyn turned to see Lynette lying on a tabletop. Brenton pressed her thighs wide as he licked her slit with a long lap that made Evelyn shiver with need. She watched his tongue retreat back into his mouth before he moved down to the opening of her pussy and stabbed his tongue into the hole. Lynette moaned as Brenton once more lapped her spread slit until he reached her clit. This time he closed his mouth around the little button and sucked.

Nigel chuckled and moved to stand by his wife's head. She cried out as her hips thrust towards Brenton's mouth. Nigel watched the pleasure ripple across her face with absolute devotion. He cupped both of her breasts and leaned down to suck on one of Lynette's nipples as her cries became frantic.

Lynette cried with her climax and Brenton sucked her clit through it. He turned his head to lock his eyes with Evelyn's while he used his thumb to rub Lynette's clit gently as she struggled to recover. Evelyn's feet moved without her brain thinking. She went to Brenton and knelt in front of him. His cock was so hard she trailed her fingers along its length in wonder for a moment before taking the head into her mouth. She licked the first drop of cum from the slit and moaned with delight.

"Suck it, Evelyn, and I'll give you the best fucking yet." She believed him too. Her pussy was screaming for it, demanding the hard erection that was filling her mouth. Evelyn could actually smell her own arousal and it mixed with the scent of Brenton's cum.

Brenton pulled her head away from his cock and lifted her from her knees a second later. He turned her around and bent her over the padded back of a sofa. "Spread your legs for me." Evelyn did and the head of his cock found her pussy. Brenton clasped her hips in his hands as he slowly pushed his length deep inside her.

Evelyn gasped at the pleasure that split her as she was impaled. Her clit was trembling with the need to climax but because Brenton was behind her, his cock wasn't sliding along the little button as he fucked her. She whimpered with the need to turn around but Brenton held her steady and continued to slowly thrust against her bottom.

"I fuck you first, Evelyn, and then last. Flatten your hands on the cushion and look at my brother." Evelyn's eyes flew open and stared into Nigel Spencer's dark ones. He held his wife against a large column just like Brenton had used the wall in her parlor to brace her back against as he fucked her standing up. Lynette's legs were twisted around her husband's waist as he thrust his cock into her spread body. Brenton moved in the same rhythm as Nigel, making her push her bottom up for the next thrust.

The only difference was Lynette was sobbing with delight because her husband's cock was rubbing her clit with each stroke. The sounds of Lynette's cries made Evelyn shiver because she understood that Nigel had the same rule. He was going to fuck his wife first, bringing her to climax before he joined Brenton in her own body.

The combination of Brenton's fucking and watching Nigel thrust into his wife held Evelyn a mere breath away from climax. It was an exquisite torment that was suspended between pain and pleasure.

Lynette cried out and her husband grinned at Evelyn as he thrust a few final times into her body. Nigel clasped his arms around his wife and gently kissed her. He carried her to a sofa and laid her on its brocade-covered surface. Lynette smiled at her husband as he turned and aimed his still erect cock in Evelyn's direction.

Chapter Eight

∞

Brenton pulled his cock from her body as Nigel moved closer. A moment later she was pressed between them both. Evelyn lost track of whose hand was where on her flesh. It all blended into a mind explosion of pleasure and sensation that surrounded the three of them. Her hands stroked and touched each set of hard shoulders. She gripped two hard cocks, one in each hand, as she turned between them. She lost one of those hard erections as Brenton moved across the room and brought two little flat-topped stools back with him. He placed them on the floor about two feet apart.

Brenton lifted her off her feet and then put one of her feet down on top of each stool. She was balanced between them with her legs spread but the stools lifted her up to a more even height with her two male companions. Nigel reached for a small wax paper packet that was lying on one of the side tables and she instantly recognized it as a sheath like the one Brenton had worn when fucking Laura.

Nigel broke the packet open and held his cock steady as he rolled the protective covering down the length of his erection. Brenton moved in front of her and cupped her face with his hands. His eyes blazed their hunger into hers a moment before he kissed her. It was a hard kiss of possession, as he pushed her lips open to demand access to her tongue. He stroked the length of her tongue with his as she felt the smooth glide of gel on her bottom. Her clit pounded with the same hard rhythm as her heart, and for a moment Evelyn wasn't sure if she would survive.

Evelyn did not care. She needed it so badly just then, that even to save her life she would not have tried to stop them. Brenton raised his head and looked into her eyes as he thrust his cock into her pussy. The hard length slid along her clit and climax ripped through her belly. Brenton held his body still as her pussy contracted around his length. Evelyn clung to his shoulders as Nigel smoothed his hands over her bottom. His breath hit her neck at the same time that Brenton laid a row of soft kisses along her cheek. They were both tender in that moment as her body lingered in the ripples of satisfaction.

Brenton moved and her clit instantly forgot about the recent pleasure. As he pulled his cock free, the hard flesh slipped along her tender flesh setting off a new round of desire. This time her bottom ached to be stretched like it had been last night.

Brenton pressed his cock back up into her and stayed embedded there as she felt Nigel move his length against the opening to her bottom. The skin protested slightly as he pulled the cheeks of her bottom apart.

A moment later he slid up into her body, pressing against the hard length lodged in her pussy. Once more she was caught between pleasure and pain, unable to distinguish one from the other. The only thought echoing inside her brain was brutal with its primitive force.

Fuck. She wanted to be fucked.

The pleasure surrounded them all, ripping into each layer of skin as Nigel pressed into her bottom and Brenton pulled his cock free. Then Nigel pulled free and Brenton was thrusting deeply into her pussy. They worked her body like that, one cock in and the other out for long moments that felt like it lasted forever. And then they both filled her at the same time and Evelyn listened to her own voice like it belonged to a stranger.

There was no holding climax off. Her clit pulsed and her body tightened around the two cocks stretching it, filling it, driving her towards rapture.

It tore her into a hundred little pieces as her body twisted, trying to get closer to both men at the same time. But it was Brenton who gathered her to his chest and caught her mouth in a tender kiss. It was his heartbeat that filled her head as she slumped against him and felt his arms take up her weight.

Of course it was Brenton—she belonged to him.

Brenton listened to Evelyn breathe. The soft sound of her little mutters of contentment was the sweetest thing he'd ever heard. He had stumbled back against a sofa and she was draped across his body as he played with her hair.

His cock was still hard and he raised a thigh to part Evelyn's. This time it was a slow thrust that sent his flesh into hers once again. The need to climax rode him hard but he didn't need to fuck her fast. No, he wanted to impale her and linger inside her gripping pussy. Just stay there and feel her flesh tighten around his until his seed was jerked up into her belly. Evelyn rolled over and lifted her eyelids to look into his eyes.

"And you fuck me last too." She whispered the words as she slipped one knee to the surface of the sofa and took up some of her own weight.

"You remember your lessons quite well." Brenton thrust up into her body as his cock tightened with the need to release its load. Evelyn watched his eyes as he sent his thumb into the front of her slit to rub over her clit.

The pleasure was deep and lingering this time. Evelyn watched Brenton's face tighten as his arms wrapped around her body to hold her against him. His seed was warm as it hit the walls of her pussy and a last rub from his thumb made her clit twist a final time with pleasure.

* * * * *

Evelyn was up with the sun. She should have been sleeping but without Brenton holding her, she could not linger in her cold bed. She frowned as the maid entered with a morning tray. She had never needed a maid before and Evelyn looked at the pillow where Brenton's head had been a mere hour past and she decided she did not need any maids now!

What she wanted was a good strong bolt installed on the door.

"Miss did not sleep well? Tea will make you smile."

Evelyn almost laughed but bit into her lower lip instead. No, tea would only make it possible for her to get what would make her happy—a good long night of fucking.

Oh my…but she certainly could not say that to the maid!

Dressing took little time and Evelyn was on the bottom floor of the house just as the morning sun was coming through the windows. She felt so alive right then, like the whole world was full of wonderful possibilities and she was going to go and grasp a few for her own happiness.

"Good morning."

A smile brightened her face as she turned to find Brenton following her down the stairs. He was dressed impeccably in a riding jacket of hunter green. A pair of gloves was actually hanging from his belt telling Eve that he was going riding, because he never wore gloves. Evelyn decided that fit him. There were a great many people who dismissed him because of his blood and they would turn their backs on her for wearing his ring.

That drove her to say yes, even harder. Not once had she encountered a finer man. Brenton cared about others and her while being honest. She would be lucky to have him for a husband but life would not be too hard for them. Brenton held the one thing that would sway most people—money. When you had as much as Brenton did, most people managed to overlook their objections to his blood.

"Come riding with me, Evelyn, let's run away before the staff get done eating their breakfast." Brenton raised his eyebrows at her as she covered her mouth with a hand to seal her amusement inside. The staff were dining in the kitchen this time of day. Brenton held out his hand and she placed hers into it as he smiled at her like a boy about to go looking for frogs in a mud hole.

Brenton took her out the side door and they dashed across the morning dew like children. The stable was musty as Brenton pulled a new quarter from his vest pocket and handed it to a groom who had two horses standing ready. The groom grunted as the money was shoved deep into his pants pocket. The man never looked at her as he handed over the reins.

"I want to show you something."

Brenton was riding just ahead of her and he motioned her to follow. Evelyn was content to go anywhere as long as she was with him. The Spencer estate was delightful and the house had fallen away behind them some time ago. Brenton rode his horse up an incline and pulled to a stop to wait for her. Evelyn looked into the valley below to discover a whole town under construction.

"This will be my new Industries in another year." Brenton's face was full of pride and he reached for the reins of her mare and took them up in his hand. He kicked his steed and they began moving down towards the unfinished buildings. Bare framing was present on what looked like dormitories. The main plant had a roof but brick was still being laid for the road that led to the large factory. As they got closer, Evelyn noticed that it was a large town, three times the size Spencer Industries was currently.

"I own this, Evelyn." Brenton's voice was filled with pride. "Every nail I bought with my own money." He turned to look at her. "There are two schoolhouses here."

Evelyn laughed. "Are you attempting to bribe me, Brenton?"

"Well, Miss Smyth, I had considered attempting to compromise your delectable person but decided I might end up as your devoted slave if I got too close to you again. So, I am shamelessly dangling my two schools in front of your nose to tempt you into marrying me."

"And then you will get to compromising my person?"

Brenton tipped his head back and roared with amusement. Evelyn giggled at the emotional display. They made a proper picture there on their horses but the subject was rather scarlet for the proper pose. That was the one thing about Brenton that delighted her the most. Moments like this were the freest ones of her entire life. It was like being let out of a cage for a single hour of sunlight and fresh air.

"Come on. Let's go explore." Brenton's face flickered with hunger as he held her mare's reins and moved his mount down the slope. Because it was Saturday, the work crew wasn't on site. Until the dormitories were complete, they would be traveling home on their off hours. That left the emerging town in eerie silence, like it had not yet been completely birthed. It had yet to take its first breath and let out a cry that said it lived.

"That will be the textile wool mill and then behind that a garment production shop for men and women." They rode right down the unpaved road that went down the center of the town. A river ran on the other side of street and there was a dock built there with a large barge moored at it. "And this is the coffee mill."

"Coffee?" Evelyn was amazed. Coffee was the biggest cash crop in the modern world right now but you had to own the tropical land that the crop was grown on.

"Yes, that's the one thing I split with a partner. Jonah Wilburn is a friend of mine who owns a little island that has some of the richest soil in the Caribbean. He grows the beans and I share my distribution lines with him."

The idea of sharing made her blush and Brenton reached across to stroke her cheek. Their eyes met in a suspended moment of remembered intimacy. Heat flickered through her pussy as she thought about once again being pressed between two men.

"Now who is making noise so god-awful early on my day of rest?" Evelyn watched as a man appeared at the gangway attached to the barge. He propped his hands onto his hips and her eyes traced the firm muscle coating his shoulders. He wore only a shirt and a pair of trousers. Rather indecent attire but ladies did not walk on the docks, that was a man's domain.

"Guess I can forgive you because you brought such a pretty present with you."

"Indeed, sir." Evelyn frowned at the presumption. She looked at Brenton. "I am not your toy."

His gloved hand cupped her chin and held it in place. "Yes, you are and you enjoy it too, but I did ask you to marry me, so simply say no if you are not in the mood today, Evelyn. I will always respect your wishes."

It amazed her to see Brenton change so quickly, from little boy to hungry male in the blink of an eye. But what shocked Evelyn the most was the way her own body responded to the flicker of hunger in his eyes. It flew across the space between them and right into her body. Her nipples drew tight beneath her corset as she felt her pussy heat with need. She moved her gaze to Jonah and let her eyes roam his frame. He stared right back at her and even grinned at her appraisal of him. He lifted one arm and extended out towards the barge behind him. He raised one light eyebrow in question at her. "I'm sure there's some lovely card games to play in the parlor if you'd like to return to the manor house."

Evelyn wrinkled her nose in response. Somehow, she doubted Lynette was dealing out sedate playing cards and she had no desire to sit at a table under the critical eye of the household staff. No, it was the truth that passion was surging through her body, pushing her towards admitting that she longed to indulge her body because who knew when the opportunity would arise once again. Tomorrow afternoon, she could climb into a carriage and return to her schoolmarm image but for now no one was watching and she was free to indulge her flesh.

Jonah laughed but it was deep and husky. His eyes were bold as Brenton reached for her waist and helped her off the mare. Evelyn lifted her chin with pride as she walked right up that gangway. She wasn't ashamed of her honesty, Brenton had taught her that. She was going to find a door and listen to the bolt slid home.

That did not make her a toy — what it made her was a woman.

Jonah's living quarters were also the bridge of his vessel. He had already yanked the curtain tassels free, washing the room in half-light. Her pussy was burning with need already. Brenton wrapped his arms around her and pressed her back against his chest. Jonah watched them as Brenton dropped a kiss onto her neck. "I would never risk you, Evelyn. Do you trust me? There are a few people who are like us — passionate. Do you know why I would get on my knees and beg you to marry me in front of a hundred ladies with fortunes? Because you know me, you are my missing half — we are two sides of a puzzle." Brenton lowered his head and inhaled her scent. "That's my way of saying I love you — everything about you."

Evelyn shivered in his embrace and he laid another kiss on her neck. Jonah watched them with an envy in his eyes and Evelyn knew at that moment he could be trusted. She saw in his eyes envy for what she and Brenton had. It was more than sexual hunger for her body, it was a emptiness that betrayed a longing for a woman who would accept him like she opened her arms to Brenton.

Reaching down, Evelyn let her hand stroke Brenton's cock through his trousers. He sucked his breath in on a harsh note as she looked at Jonah while she did it. The need to fuck was building in her, burning away her tolerance for clothing. She wanted to tear at her buttons and hooks until she was free to feel.

Brenton's hands found the top button of her jacket and opened it. Jonah's eyes were like slaves that followed Brenton's hands as they opened her riding jacket. He peeled the open garment over her shoulders and down her arms. Jonah moved forward and stroked the swells of her breasts with his fingers then kissed each breast before he took a deep breath next to her skin.

"God, you smell good woman." Jonah raised his eyes to hers as his hands found the first hook on her corset. He snapped it open as Brenton's fingers worked the hooks on her skirt. Her garments were soon a puddle on the wooden floor as the morning air brushed her nude body. Two pairs of hands stroked and moved over her body, flooding her with sensation.

"Your cunt smells so hot." Jonah dropped to his knees and parted her thighs with his hands. He looked right at her pussy as he groaned. "I'm a blunt man, Evelyn. I like pussy, the way it smells, the way it tastes and the way it feels around my cock." Brenton still stood behind her, pressing her forward as Jonah sent a finger into her slit. There was a little wet sound as he pulled his finger free and then thrust it into her slit once again. This time he made contact with her clit. Pleasure spiked up into her pussy as he drew his finger out of her slit.

A little whimper rose from her throat and Jonah looked up her body to grin at her. "Like that do you? Good." Jonah sat down on the floor and pulled her to her knees with him. His hands cupped her bottom as he lay completely on his back and pulled her down until she was kneeling right over his face. Her knees were on either side of his shoulders, spreading her pussy wide and Jonah took instant advantage. His tongue lapped across her slit and flickered over her clit as Evelyn cried out. Jonah groaned and sucked her clit into his mouth. Pleasure spiked into her pussy as Evelyn fought to hold her body upright.

Brenton stepped in front of her as she panted, and his clothing was gone. His cock thrust up in the dim light as he caught her head with his hands and offered it to her mouth. "Suck me, Evelyn."

Jonah growled around her clit and she gasped. Brenton thrust his cock into her open mouth as she gripped onto his flanks to steady her body. Jonah flicked his tongue over her clit as the man growled some more. Vibrations from his mouth added to the motions of his tongue and her clit twisted as climax ripped into her. Brenton grunted with approval as he fucked her mouth with his cock.

"Damn fine cunt." Jonah whistled softly as he sent his finger up into her pussy. Evelyn sucked hard on Brenton's cock but he held her head back with her hair and pulled his length from her mouth. Little wet sounds filled the room as Jonah used his fingers to penetrate her pussy. He rubbed her clit with his thumb and then pulled her back down to lap her entire slit from pussy to clit.

"I could eat that for an hour."

Brenton growled and lifted her from her knees. He swung her up and cradled her against his bare chest. He turned around and lowered her to her feet facing a small writing table. The surface was only a foot wide and Brenton bent her over the little, flat surface. "Put your hands down and spread your legs for me." Need coated his words as Evelyn flattened her hands on the tabletop and moved her feet apart. Brenton hooked an arm around her waist and used his free hand to guide his cock to the opening of her pussy.

His penetration felt so good, even in spite of her climax. She needed to be filled and he thrust up into her body, stretching her pussy with his cock. Brenton fucked her hard, each thrust making her body jerk forward as he rammed his length, balls-deep into her pussy.

Jonah suddenly appeared in front of her and his clothing was gone as well. In his hand his cock was swollen and crowned with a ruby head. He offered it to her lips as Brenton fucked her from behind. Evelyn sucked on his cock as Brenton slapped her bottom. Her clit throbbed but climax was out of reach because his cock wasn't sliding along her clit as he fucked. It didn't matter, it felt so good to be full and Jonah's cock tasted good as she let her tongue draw a harsh grunt from the man.

"Enough!" Jonah pulled his cock away as he looked at Brenton. "I want to come in her pussy."

"Yes!" Evelyn sobbed the word because her clit begged for release. Brenton's cock pulled free of her body and then he lifted her over the table so that she sat on it. Jonah spread her thighs with his hips as his cock found her pussy. She climaxed almost instantly. A low moan filling the room as Jonah cussed and his seed spilled into her as she felt her pussy contracting around his cock.

They were a tangle of limbs but Evelyn floated on little ripples of rapture as Brenton scooped her off the table and took her to the bed. He lay down on top of her and thrust back into her body as he stretched her arms above her head and rode her with hard thrusts. It was deep and slow and her clit twisted tighter with each stroke of his cock. Brenton watched her the entire time and when she climaxed his eyes flared with a fire so intense it burned her as well.

She slept between them both, her head pillowed on Brenton's shoulder as Jonah stroked her hip with one large hand. Right? Wrong? It just felt complete.

* * * * *

"If you don't marry me, Evelyn, I will never bring you here again."

Evelyn gasped. Oh, sweet temptation. Brenton offered her a smirk of boyish mischief over his cards as he laid one down on the parlor table.

"I might make a dreadfully demanding wife." Nigel choked and Lynette hit her husband with her fan.

Brenton raise a dark eyebrow. "I will do my best to please you, Evelyn, if you but give me the chance."

Oh Lord help her…she loved him.

It was more than that. Evelyn was filled with an amazing glow of contentment that Brenton truly did not care to further his fortune by hunting for the right bride. He wanted her because they could feed each other's hungers. Money could not buy what they sparked in each other. He was a man who would serve his principles before the bottom line. He was a man that she could pledge her life to and cheerfully face the unknown of the future with him.

"I will marry you, Brenton, but only because I believe I love you."

Brenton leaned across the table to whisper, his eyes shimmering with unshed tears as he stroked her cheek with the back of his hand. "I don't just love you, Evelyn, I crave you. I think you must be a witch because you cast a spell on me the first moment I laid eyes on you. Love? It seems a little too small a word to describe my feelings for you."

Brenton led her back towards her room that night but he did not leave her. He rolled right into the larger bed and clasped her to his chest. Evelyn giggled as she considered the maid who would walk right into the room in a few short hours to open the shades.

The dear girl was in for a shock. But then Evelyn herself was rather shocked. Love was the greatest of mysteries, it materialized when you least expected it and simply refused to budge.

How very fitting that it came in the form of Brenton Ashton. The man was completely stubborn when it came to gaining compliance from her. She was going to have to see to schooling the man — personally.

It just might take a lifetime together. Fifty years of lessons. Evelyn was looking forward to the improper ones!

* * * * *

They arrived back at Spencer Industries as man and wife. The good wives all dabbed at their eyes as Brenton swept his hat off and introduced her as Mrs. Ashton. The men nodded their heads with approval because a married schoolmarm was even more respectable than the well-referenced one they had gained the week before.

The Princeton agency was thrilled and added another shining example to their list of achievements. Brenton had taken her to City Hall to file the marriage paperwork before he allowed her out of his sight.

He had moved right into her little apartment. His sleeping rooms had backed up to another overseer's rooms and the schoolhouse offered more privacy for new lovers. Small was fine because Evelyn needed to be close to her husband. They worked as hard as they played and that was the way she intended to keep it.

* * * * *

Her wedding ring caught the sunlight as Evelyn pulled the rope to ring the school bell on Monday morning. Her husband watched from his office as children left their chores to run towards the rows of desks where the future was being unlocked for their little eyes.

Life was full of lessons and Evelyn appreciated each and every one of them!

Appearances were being maintained with her somber schoolmarm dress and tightly pinned braids, but hidden beneath her skirt was a pair of black stockings drawn around her thighs with purple ribbons. No one needed to know that her knickers were in the bottom drawer of her dresser. Well, no one save her husband, that was!

After all, she needed to keep up appearances with Brenton as well.

Lessons…life was full of them and Evelyn admitted she enjoyed the pursuit of knowledge.

Enjoy An Excerpt From:

IMPROPER LONGINGS

Her lower lip was so dry, Charity licked it. The wet contact shocked her with its pure carnal feeling. Her face flamed with a blush as she pressed her palm against the hot surface of her cheek. A little moan surfaced from her throat as the vision of Gaea and her lover replayed across her memory. She left the room and dashed across the hallway into another room as she wrung her hands.

Charity considered the horror of being honest enough to admit that she could not have torn her eyes from the spectacle for anything. She had wanted to watch. Practically needed to end her ignorance of just exactly what the marriage bed would offer her.

And so she had.

She licked her lips once more as she moved around the small room. Sunlight filtered through the reed shades covering the windows but she didn't need the afternoon sun to heat her face. A deep male chuckle met her ears and she froze, each and every muscle drew taut before she turned around to discover Jonah watching her with his dark eyes.

"Well, that was a bit of an education for you, I'll wager." He chuckled once more as his gaze lingered on her scarlet cheeks.

"Indeed."

Jonah considered her face a moment as her comment sunk in. Instead of an indignant tone, she'd delivered that single word in a sort of curious whisper. That snared his attention. Her white cotton dress was buttoned primly to her neck and her face was bright red, but she wasn't shocked. Her nose wasn't wrinkled into disgust or her lips twisted by a disapproving frown. His cock twitched once again and this time the demanding flesh wasn't interested in dismissing anything about sweet Charity. Beneath her lady's exterior lay a woman who was quite bold.

He never could ignore a bold female, it was his fatal weakness. Some men were drawn to the whisky bottle. He was a slave to carnal pleasure. But it was a lot easier to find a bar than a passionate partner. A whore wasn't the same thing. She was paid to spread her thighs. What Jonah craved was a lover who would cling to him as devotedly as he would hold on to her.

"I should go."

Jonah raised an eyebrow at her. "Why? Because you're honest with yourself and admit you watched? Not anything wrong with that. Leastways, not as far as I'm concerned." Jonah watched for her response, there was a devil pulling on his brain, tempting him to encourage Charity to abandon her prim and proper teachings. Oh she'd been reared as a lady no doubt, but somehow she'd escaped the strangling hold the current society managed to wrap around its women. She wasn't afraid of her own body and that sent a surge of heat straight into his cock. "Seems sort of in character for you."

"And what does that mean?"

Now she was offended. Jonah chuckled again at the spark of hunger edging her voice. "I mean that you're no simpleton who just accepts what she's told. Admit it, Charity, hidden beneath that unruly mass of hair is a mind that you don't allow to be idle."

"Of course not." But that didn't mean that watching Gaea consort with Teo was the kind of observation she should be engaging in. Jonah considered her face for a moment.

"So what if you enjoyed watching. All that means is you're healthy."

Her face creased into a frown as she considered his comment. It wasn't something he should have said to her but he just couldn't resist. His cock was hard and aching for her to abandon more of society and its idiotic rules. They were both healthy adults and the blunt fact was, he wanted to shove up inside her. But he wanted her to crave it as much as he did. Jonah chuckled as he contemplated the best method of seduction.

"Despite what society might like to preach, sex is healthy. We'd be extinct otherwise."

"That doesn't mean it is correct." Charity frowned again as she listened to her own voice. She sounded disappointed, a lot like a child being denied a sweet plainly sitting in sight. "You have a way of twisting words, Jonah."

"I'm untwisting them." He moved across the room and caught her chin in his hand again. "What's the terrible sin in admitting that humans enjoy mating? It's a necessary part of life, even encouraged by the church. Why can't you enjoy it?"

"Good question." Gaea certainly looked like she enjoyed it. Charity licked her lower lip once more as she considered her own body. She did like the way Jonah's hand felt against her face. Her nipples were tingling as she longed for him to touch her exactly as Teo had stroked Gaea.

"Isn't it?" Jonah caught her mouth in a kiss. Her lips parted beneath his as memory filled her with how much pleasure she'd found in his embrace last night. His hand slipped around to the back of her head to hold it steady as his tongue stroked her lower lip. His tongue felt better than hers had on the delicate flesh. His other hand lay against her lower back but today he stepped right up against her body and used that hand to hold her in position. The hard shape of his cock pressed against her belly, and she shuddered as she recognized exactly what the flesh was used for now. Jonah left her mouth and trailed his lips down the side of her neck, making her shiver as sensation flowed into her sex. Her nipples twisted tighter behind her corset as her ungloved hands spread out over his shoulders.

"What's so wrong with touching? I love the way you feel against my body."

"We're not married."

Jonah found the first button on the front of her top and separated it. He stroked the newly bared skin with a fingertip before reaching for the next button.

"Would that change whether or not you like my touch?"

Charity shook her head. Jonah undid the next button and another as he sent his hand towards her waist. She should protest but it felt too good to offer him false protest. "It would change how another man viewed me though."

"Some men are idiots."

"I would think the word 'possessive' is a better one." Jonah stroked the top of one breast and she lost interest in any sort of conversation that took their attention from touching. It simply felt so very good. "I would have married years ago if I knew it would feel like this."

Jonah growled at her. Charity opened her eyes and faced a hard expression that she had never seen Jonah display before. Clearly he did not like her thinking that any man would do. Jealousy flickered in his eyes as he looked at her.

Why an electronic book?

We live in the Information Age—an exciting time in the history of human civilization, in which technology rules supreme and continues to progress in leaps and bounds every minute of every day. For a multitude of reasons, more and more avid literary fans are opting to purchase e-books instead of paper books. The question from those not yet initiated into the world of electronic reading is simply: *Why?*

1. ***Price.*** An electronic title at Ellora's Cave Publishing and Cerridwen Press runs anywhere from 40% to 75% less than the cover price of the exact same title in paperback format. Why? Basic mathematics and cost. It is less expensive to publish an e-book (no paper and printing, no warehousing and shipping) than it is to publish a paperback, so the savings are passed along to the consumer.

2. ***Space.*** Running out of room in your house for your books? That is one worry you will never have with electronic books. For a low one-time cost, you can purchase a handheld device specifically designed for e-reading. Many e-readers have large, convenient screens for viewing. Better yet, hundreds of titles can be stored within your new library—on a single microchip. There are a variety of e-readers from different manufacturers. You can also read e-books on your PC or laptop computer. (Please note that Ellora's Cave does not endorse any specific brands. You can check our websites at www.ellorascave.com

or www.cerridwenpress.com for information we make available to new consumers.)

3. *Mobility.* Because your new e-library consists of only a microchip within a small, easily transportable e-reader, your entire cache of books can be taken with you wherever you go.

4. *Personal Viewing Preferences.* Are the words you are currently reading too small? Too large? Too... ANNOYING? Paperback books cannot be modified according to personal preferences, but e-books can.

5. *Instant Gratification.* Is it the middle of the night and all the bookstores near you are closed? Are you tired of waiting days, sometimes weeks, for bookstores to ship the novels you bought? Ellora's Cave Publishing sells instantaneous downloads twenty-four hours a day, seven days a week, every day of the year. Our webstore is never closed. Our e-book delivery system is 100% automated, meaning your order is filled as soon as you pay for it.

Those are a few of the top reasons why electronic books are replacing paperbacks for many avid readers.

As always, Ellora's Cave and Cerridwen Press welcome your questions and comments. We invite you to email us at Comments@ellorascave.com or write to us directly at Ellora's Cave Publishing Inc., 1056 Home Avenue, Akron, OH 44310-3502.

THE
⚱ ELLORA'S CAVE ⚱
LIBRARY

Stay up to date with Ellora's Cave Titles in
Print with our Quarterly Catalog.

To recieve a catalog,
send an email with your name
and mailing address to:

CATALOG@ELLORASCAVE.COM
or send a letter or postcard
with your mailing address to:

Catalog Request
c/o Ellora's Cave Publishing, Inc.
1056 Home Avenue
Akron, Ohio 44310-3502

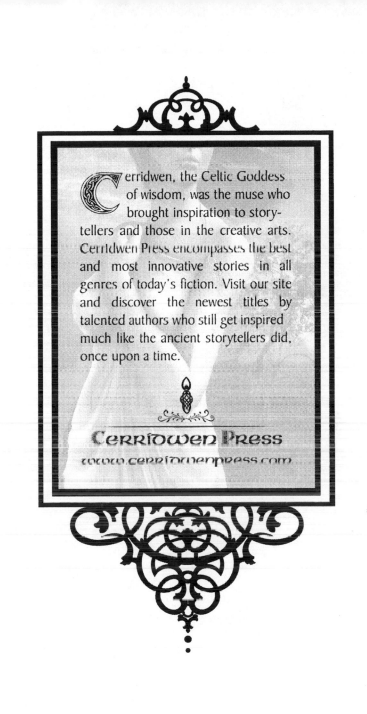

erridwen, the Celtic Goddess of wisdom, was the muse who brought inspiration to storytellers and those in the creative arts. Cerridwen Press encompasses the best and most innovative stories in all genres of today's fiction. Visit our site and discover the newest titles by talented authors who still get inspired much like the ancient storytellers did, once upon a time.

Cerridwen Press

www.cerridwenpress.com

Discover for yourself why readers can't get enough
of the multiple award-winning publisher

Ellora's Cave.

Whether you prefer e-books or paperbacks,

be sure to visit EC on the web at
www.ellorascave.com

for an erotic reading experience that will leave you
breathless.